KU-561-374

Traps & Pelts

Arthur Joseph Fry

authorHOUSE™
1663 Liberty Drive, Suite 200
Bloomington, Indiana 47403
(800) 839-8640
www.AuthorHouse.com

This book is a work of fiction. People, places, events, and situations are the product of the author's imagination. Any resemblance to actual persons, living or dead, or historical events, is purely coincidental.

First published by AuthorHouse 12/14/05

ISBN: 1-4208-8698-3 (sc)

Printed in the United States of America

Bloomington, Indiana

This book is printed on acid-free paper.

DEDICATION

To my wife, Nora, who encouraged and inspired me to write this book.

CONTENTS

CHAPTER ONE
OLAF'S DREAM

The mid-afternoon sun hovered like a fire-ball in the endless blue sky and radiated a blazing heat throughout the valley. Such an intense summer had not been experienced in Norway for at least twenty years. Olaf Svenson remembers his father talking about that summer. Perspiration trickled down his forehead and into his eyes faster than could be wiped away with his neck scarf. The rest of his body was soaked with moisture and he felt uncomfortable. Olaf worked the farm with his father, mother and two brothers. The dairy farm provided a reasonable living for the family of five, but Olaf had a passionate desire to do something more than just work on the farm. He had a need to branch out and direct his life on a course that was more exciting and challenging than staying at home.

That evening, Olaf invited his family to gather in the cool shade at the side of the old log house. Here he expressed his desire to leave the farm in order to fulfil a dream to emigrate to Canada and start a new life.

What kind of life it would be, he did not know at the moment. He only knew that he must go and experience a different life. At first the family were all surprised and emotional about his decision and presented barriers as to why he should not leave. His mother was tearful and begged him to reconsider. As well, his brothers tried to persuade him to stay. How could they run the farm without him? Eventually, Olaf's dad spoke. Gustav said that he can relate to Olaf's desire to leave and, if he feels strongly to do so, he should. He talked about the time when he wanted to leave home, his family emotionally blackmailed him by making him feel guilty for wanting to go. So, he stayed, but in his heart he felt a great sorrow and disappointment. Olaf was overjoyed with his father's blessing. The rest of the family then understood his need and, as well, gave him their blessings. Helga, his mother, though still emotional over his decision, agreed that if that's what he desires, so be it.

The following day, Olaf began preparations. He packed his clothing and personal belongings into two suitcases and a small trunk. The next day he spent, in Christiania, now Oslo, getting his passport in order, sea trip booked and finances arranged with his bank. He will carry a substantial amount of cash as well as a bank draft in Canadian funds. His journey was scheduled to start in eight days. He would go by rail to the port at Bergen and board the boat to South Hampton, England, from which an Ocean Liner will transport him to Montreal, Canada. It seemed an eternity for the eight days to go by. Eventually, the time for departure arrived. After hugs, kisses, well wishes and promises to write, he boarded the rickety, old bus to Bergen.

The four-week voyage was uneventful and relaxing. During the voyage, Olaf met a fellow countryman, Stefan Yorgi, who also was going to Canada. His new found acquaintance revealed that he was going to northern Manitoba to try his hand at fur trapping. It was a good, but hard life, with the chance of making a very good living. The prospect of doing the same was challenging and exciting to Olaf. He never was one to be put off with hard work. The vocation of a fur trapper was the type of adventure he inwardly sought. July 30, 1920, the boat docked at Montreal. A hum of excitement and anticipation was in the air as the passengers disembarked. For Olaf, it was the beginning of his long, cherished dream. After clearing customs, the two men found their way to a hotel where they indulged themselves in fine food and a night out on the town. Such luxuries would be the last they would enjoy for a long time.

The following day they arranged train passage to Winnipeg, Manitoba. This would be a three-day journey through some of the most beautiful countryside in Canada. That evening, they boarded the train carrying hand luggage containing their toiletries and some clothing. The cases and trunks were checked into the baggage car and wouldn't be seen until they arrive in Winnipeg. The porter directed them to their berths and the dining room. The train rumbled its way across the land through well-groomed farmland before entering the forested areas further north. There were many ponds, lakes and rushing rivers to be seen as the train sped resolutely northward. At night, the lamps of farmhouses and log cabins poked yellow rays of light through tiny windows. The berths were not comfortable due to hard mattresses and the constant swaying of the sleeping car. On the other hand, the dining room meals made up for the sleeping discomforts. The meals were plain and wholesome, what they were accustomed to at home. The journey in itself was boring after one had absorbed much of the scenery, which began to take on a sameness all along. However, meeting and talking to other passengers did help fill in the time. Whenever the train made a stop at a town or settlement, it was enjoyable to get out and stretch their legs and view the local residents who ritually met the train, regardless of the time. As the train neared a large community, the conductor passed through the coaches announcing that the next stop was Winnipeg and there would be a half-hour stopover while the engine took on water and coal. The train chugged into the station and came to a squealing stop. The old, dusty engine stood like a tired dragon, puffing, hissing and belching black clouds of suffocating smoke across the platform. Olaf and Stefan disembarked and retrieved their belongings from the baggage car. An arrangement was made with the station porter to have them stored in the luggage shed. They hired transport for themselves to a hotel in downtown Winnipeg, a burgeoning city. The hotel was not as comfortable and lavish as the one in Montreal, but being raised in a rustic environment, they were not bothered about not having a luxurious suite in which to languish.

Olaf and Stefan wakened from a deep, refreshing sleep and agreed that, compared to the train berths, these beds were akin to sleeping on air. There was not a cloud in the sky and by mid-morning the temperature was hovering in the seventy-degree range. The two men wolfed down a full breakfast of bacon, sausage, eggs, toast, jam and coffee. Fully fortified, they eagerly set out to locate the Manitoba Lands and Forest Service to arrange for trapping permits and to determine the areas in which they would be allowed to trap. Olaf was informed that a trapper, who had died two years ago, previously held the area assigned to him. Thus, it not having been worked for that period, it was a likely-hood that the animals will have increased in number. Unfortunately, the areas assigned to Olaf and Stefan were not close to each other. A distance of two hundred and forty miles would separate them, which rules out periodic visits. However, life must go on and there was much to prepare for the adventurous and unknown future ahead.

The remainder of the day and most of the next were busy in procuring necessary supplies from the Northern Supply Company. Food staples, tools, rifles, ammunition, building hardware, broad axes, nails, bucksaw and blades, spade, first aide supplies and medications, traps, fishing gear, hip waders, snowshoes, sufficient suitable clothing, several pairs of comfortable, warm leather bush boots, needles and strong thread, matches, candles, three kerosene lamps and fuel, a portable tin, camp stove and chimney pipes, reading material, a sturdy, twenty-foot canvas covered canoe with four paddles and repair materials and a host of other sundries made up the required needs. When stacked, the respective piles of gear resembled two miniature mountains. All of these supplies were to be delivered to the Canadian National Railway depot for shipment to the town of Winnipegosis, on Lake Winnipegosis, the end of the line and then flown to their respective lakes. At this point, Olaf and Stefan would part and not see each other for many years. At the bank they opened an account and deposited the remaining portion of their money they would not need in the north. They would rely on procuring needed goods from the Hudson's Bay Trading Posts with cheques.

Their last evening together was spent leisurely. The night was warm. They strolled about and enjoyed the quiet stillness of the city. They talked about their futures and wondered what life would be like in isolation. Each expressed his fears and hopes, but not once did they indicate any doubts about the course they chose. They promised to write whenever it was possible to get a letter sent out. Completely exhausted by the activities of the last two days, they were ready for a good night's sleep. At the first light of day they had to pack, have breakfast, checkout and be down to the train depot prior to eight o'clock. While buying their tickets, the station master informed them that their outfits were already loaded and they must be certain to check the unloading of them at their destination. Personal luggage in hand, Olaf and Stefan boarded the train for the trip to the northern reaches beyond.

The ancient, chugging engine roughly tugged at its motley collection of passenger, baggage and freight cars as it lumbered, swayed and rattled its way along the spindly, rail artery to the north. Black smoke belched from the stack and choking clouds of soot would be sucked into the passenger cars when the doors between them were opened, and, as the day progressed, windows that were opened due to the heat and stuffiness, allowed more smoke to enter the cars. The seats were covered with a film of black grime that had to be wiped away before sitting. At one end of each passenger car there was a cast-iron, pot-bellied stove which was the source of heat during the late fall and winter. The leather covered seats were worn and shoddy due to the hundreds of bodies that had occupied them over the years.

Each passenger car had a washroom with a toilet and sink. There was no dining room or catering service on this run. Passengers had to bring their own lunches, enough to sustain them for the trip. At night, when the kerosene lamps were turned down low, the passengers made themselves as comfortable as possible, sitting up or slouching to fit their bodies comfortably into the contours of the seats. Throughout the night, sonorous sounds emanated from the throats and noses of the sleepers. Occasionally the train would lurch as the engine put on a burst of speed, causing some to waken with a start. The cast of passengers was a mixture of races. There were German, Norwegian, English, French, American and Native persons travelling, a blend of farmers, trappers, and settlers. The travellers occupied themselves in various ways to escape the boredom of the journey. Some slept, some read, some walked about, some played cards and others were deeply engaged in conversation. The Indians sat stoically looking out the window. Thus, the trip was endured. Day blended into night and night into day.

The scenery changed as the train progressed steadily northward. Leaving Winnipeg, the landscape was a panorama of cultivated fields and established farms. The crops of grain were coming into their own, golden yellow, standing erect and swaying gently in the breeze. Mounds of sun cured hay dotted the shorn fields like golden dollops of ice-cream sitting on a large, flat, ochre coloured plate. Cattle browsed and at times gazed blankly at the train as it passed. In other fields, horses were grazing lazily and some were rolling on their backs in the dusty soil, legs thrashing the empty air as though they were swatting flies.

Soon the dense forested regions of pine, poplar and hardwood trees replaced the flatlands. A labyrinth of rough, tracked roads snaked their way from the railroad and disappeared into a mass of trees. Along the way, small, wooden shacks and old log cabins were haphazardly spaced at various distances from the tracks. These housed the loners who lived in isolation, trying to eke out a living from cutting trees for the lumber companies or trapping. The children and adults, who stood to watch the train trundle by, looked the picture of abject poverty. The region through which they were now travelling contained many small lakes and potholes. The land surface was spongy and slight undulations of the tracks could be felt while sitting or walking about. Small wooden bridges crossed over minor rivers and streams that permeated the area. Olaf and Stefan felt the excitement mount in their veins.

Some short stops were made along the way to dislodge passengers and supplies and, at times, a lone trapper waved the train down to receive groceries and mail or possibly to load himself and his bundle of furs, destined to be traded at the Hudson's Bay Post further north. Large conifer trees, lakes and fast flowing rivers made up the landscape. Beaver lodges and muskrat hills dotted many of the ponds. Moose were browsing in the shallow waters of the lakes. These creatures appeared ungainly, but when startled, they trotted away with the speed and the grace of a ballerina. Timid white-tailed deer, their tails flicking nervously, eyed the train as it jostled along and stood poised, ready to leap to the safety of the trees. The train laboriously lumbered over the ribbons of steel and as it neared Winipegosis, signs of civilization became more prevalent. Shacks and log cabins began to come into view and many dirt trails and deeply rutted roads, showing signs of much human and animal traffic, led off into the forest. The engineer pulled the whistle cord and several shrill blasts penetrated the still, afternoon air. As the engine cruised to a stop, a hive of humanity crowded the platform, all eager to receive friends, relatives and view the strangers getting off. The station crew worked quickly to unload the baggage car and load the contents onto the luggage wagons to transport them to the station storage room.

As Olaf and Stefan stepped from the train they saw what seemed to be the entire populace of Winnipegosis milling about like ants on a hill. They looked at each other and spontaneously grinned and laughed loudly. Their dreams were now closer to fulfilment. With the Station master, the men made arrangements to leave their goods secured in the storage room overnight. They learned that the air Transport Company was located at the bottom of Hill Road. Immediately, they made their way to the docks to arrange transportation north. Olaf's trapping region was on Wekusko Lake, about one hundred and fifty air miles northwest of Winnipegosis. Stefan's area was located on Morrison Lake, approximately one hundred and ten miles northeast. The dispatcher arranged for the men to be flown into their respective trapping areas on the following day. They were to have all their gear down to the docks by 11:00 a.m., ready to be loaded onto the planes. Olaf's flight was to leave at noon and Stefan's at 1:30 p.m.

The friends then made their way to the to the village to find some lodging for the night. Winnipegosis was the typical northern settlement. It consisted of weathered, board homes and businesses, looking like so many grey, wooden boxes standing side by side. A few log homes were interspersed amongst them. They walked up the dusty road called Main Street to the hotel. It was a two-storey edifice that resembled those seen in the western movies. They carefully climbed the wobbly steps and crossed the creaky, warped boards of the veranda and entered the main room through a door loosely supported by rusty hinges that squealed in protest whenever it was opened. Inside, the appearance was in no way indicative of what the outside portrayed.

The lobby was tastefully appointed, as well as could be expected in the rugged north. To one side of the log reception desk were two sofas and three leather chairs arranged in a half circle in front of a huge, fieldstone fireplace above which hung the huge head of what was once a magnificent bull moose. Its beady eyes glared fiercely down at the guests sitting around reading, talking or enjoying a drink and a cigar. There was a door on each side of the lobby, one led off into the lounge and the other into the dining room. To the right of the reception desk a wide stairway led to the upper bedroom chambers.

For a very reasonable price Olaf and Stefan procured a room with two single beds, dinner and breakfast included. The room was clean and spacious. The walls were covered over with a vivid blue, green and red paisley pattern. A threadbare, green rug covered the floor which quietly complained when walked across. The bed and furniture pieces were old but quite functional as such. The shared bathroom and wash facilities were at the end of the long, dimly lit corridor. After freshening up, they casually strolled down to the dining room for the evening meal which featured moose steak or stew, boiled potatoes, canned corn, wild Saskatoon Berry pie and copious amounts of strong coffee, laced with concentrated canned milk.

Completely sated and refreshed, they sauntered about the town. They visited the general store and purchased some last minute articles to carry with them; candies, pipe and tobacco, extra matches, soap and a straight razor with a honing strap. Darkness had stealthily crept down on the landscape and the village was bathed in a ghostly glow from the light of the full moon which floated in a cloudless sky above the lake. A gentle, cool breeze was blowing through the settlement, promising a comfortable night's sleep after the searing heat of the day. As the two friends slowly walked to their hotel, they reminisced about their meeting, their plans and indefinite future. As they lay in their beds and talked across to each other, sleep overcame them and forced its will; soon both were in a deep slumber.

Being farm bred, they were used to waking early without an alarm clock. By seven thirty, breakfast was over. They checked out and made their way to the train depot to arrange the delivery of their goods to the dock. The station master was most helpful. He obtained the services of a local citizen who owned a horse and wagon. In no time they had everything piled on the dock, ready to be loaded. Olaf's belongings were put on board first and within the hour his flight was ready to leave. The friends emotionally hugged and shook hands. Tears started to sneak down the sides of their cheeks causing them to feel embarrassed. Olaf boarded the plane with sadness in his heart, but also, he was excited about making the last leg of his journey to where he must face the unknown and rely on his personal skills, reasoning, stamina, faith and inner spirit to survive. As the plane taxied from the dock, Olaf looked back and slowly waved to his friend.

CHAPTER TWO
SETTLING IN

The pilot, Jim Barnes, eased the plane smoothly from the dock into open water. The engine was turning over quietly as he nosed out and faced into the wind. Momentarily there was a slight hesitation just before Jim opened the throttle wide. The craft picked up speed and raced down the waterway until the floats were skimming along the top of the water and then it gracefully ascended into the blue sky. Olaf saw his friend standing on the dock, waving. He watched until Stefan was just a dot on the landing. Ahead was the open blue sky with bunches of fluffy, white clouds floating lazily before a gentle wind. Lake Winnipegosis looked like a sapphire gem, with dazzling reflections from the sun. Tiny islands, resembling green quilt patches of different hues, placed randomly on a blue background, were dotted about its surface. Soon, the expansive lake was left behind and they were flying over the endless dense forested regions.

The two men talked about things in general. Olaf spoke about his life of twenty-three years on the farm in

Norway and about his dream to realize a different life from what he had with his family. Jim remarked that Olaf had a good command of the English Language. Olaf replied that he learned it in high school as a second language and was able to practise it on the tourists that came to Christiania. Jim said that a Scotsman, Angus McGregor, who died of pneumonia two winters back, trapped the area to which he was going. Also, the cabin, which he had built, is still standing and in reasonable condition.

He said that he had landed there occasionally to look things over and it would be a shame for Olaf not to take it over, because it would, in time, deteriorate through neglect. The stove needed new pipes, otherwise it was in good order. The table, chairs, bunk bed and shelves need some reinforcing to bring them back to a sturdy state. Besides, it would be nick and tuck to build and finish a cabin before the cold winter gripped the land. Olaf could not believe his luck. He was highly delighted to have a home to move into immediately, thus the time saved in not having to build could be devoted to laying out his trap lines and learning about his area. Olaf felt extremely good about how events have progressed since he left home. The pilot announced that they were nearing Wekusko Lake and should arrive there in fifteen minutes. The minutes could not pass quickly enough for Olaf. He was anxious to see the lake from the air. Suddenly it was below them.

Jim flew the entire course of the lake and pointed out

many of the landmarks that would be helpful to Olaf. The lake was about thirty-five miles long and twenty miles wide. They passed over the Hudson's Bay Trading Post at Hall's Landing situated at the extreme south end of the lake. Jim then swung the aircraft around and within moments descended to the mouth of Grass River where Olaf would be living for the next few years. As they were coming in to land, Olaf quickly scanned the entire area and was delighted to see the lonely cabin, nestled amidst the trees on an embankment overlooking the lake, as if it was an old friend waiting to greet him. A trail edged its way up from a sandy beach and found its way to the door of the cabin. The plane touched down onto the water and gently eased up to the beach. The motor was shut off and it protested with a splutter and a cough before coming to a stop. Jim hastily jumped out and tied the plane to a towering pine tree that stood like a sentinel on guard. The afternoon was slipping by and the men worked steadily to unload all the gear in order for Jim to be on his way long before the veil of darkness closed over the land.

The canoe, securely lashed to the struts of the right pontoon, was the first item to be unloaded. This was an easy task, because when it was untied, it slid into the lake and floated to shore. Piece by piece, the gear was laboriously unloaded and carried to a dry spot on the beach. This chore lasted an hour. Jim was able to spare a little time, before leaving, to give assistance in lugging the heavier pieces up to the cabin. The rest would be up to Olaf to struggle with.

As he boarded the plane, Jim said that whenever he was in the area he would drop by to see how things were going and asked if there was anything special he would like to have him bring. Some tobacco and reading material would be appreciated was the reply. Olaf released the anchor rope and shoved the plane from shore into deeper water. The engine sputtered and then exploded into action causing the propeller to whirl rapidly. The propeller and motor smoothly synchronized into the idling mode. Jim throttled the motor into taxiing speed and glided the craft into the main lake. The aircraft roared its way down Wekusko Lake and lifted from the water as though it were catapulted into the air by an unseen force. With a wiggle of the wings, the Otter Craft droned off into the distance.

With some apprehension and a feeling of loneliness, Olaf turned to survey the remainder of the supplies piled haphazardly on the white sand. He thought it best to remove all the goods to the cabin before doing anything else. Eventually, after much struggling and sweating, all was stored safely inside the cabin. During this task, thick, grey clouds began to pile up in the formidable looking sky and a stiff breeze whipped off the lake. Suddenly, with a fierce, bright streak of lightning and a thunderous clap, the sky opened up and a deluge obliterated the landscape. If the rain had come a half-hour sooner, the situation would have been in dire straits. Now, before complete darkness fell, he had to rummage around to find the supply of candles to afford him some kind of illumination. He was thankful that the outfitting store listed the contents of the boxes on the lids. The candles were located and several were lit and strategically placed around the cabin. A quick glance about the dusky cabin assured Olaf that it would be an adequate home away from home. Tomorrow will be a day of cleaning up and putting things in order. That evening, his meal consisted of cold beans and several hardtack biscuits. He tidied up the makeshift bunk and unrolled the sleeping bag along its length. The candles were snuffed out and he removed his boots and collapsed, fully clothed, into his bag, completely exhausted. As sleep slowly crept into his brain, he was aware of the rain pummelling the roof and the drip, drip of a leak.

As the morning light stealthily crept in through the grimy windows, Olaf was awakened from the slumber of the dead by sounds of tiny scurrying feet, interjected with squeaks, which meant that he had unwanted roommates. Quickly he stomped his feet onto the floor and gave chase to the rodents who quickly disappeared into the holes and crevices of the cabin wall. The rain had stopped during the night and the morning air was fresh and cool. This was a welcomed contrast to the blistering heat of the past few day.

After a scant breakfast of unappetizing hardtack and jam, he commenced to clean up the debris from two years of un-occupancy. Dust, mouse droppings and old garbage had to be done away with. The furniture, bunk bed and shelves were repaired and strengthened. He replaced the stovepipes with those he brought for his portable camp stove. The firebox was swept clean of soot and old ashes. Clean sand, from the beach, was placed in the box surrounding the stove. This was to prevent the heat from burning the floor. Gradually, he was able to store his supplies and gear on the shelves and elsewhere about the cabin. Old MacGregor had kept an odd assortment of old rusty tin containers in which dried goods were stored to prevent the furry squatters from getting into them. These were used to great advantage.

The floor was made of puncheons, sturdy half logs with the smooth sides up. The glass windowpanes were given a quick wipe. One had cracked across the centre, but it remained in place. Some work was needed to make the panes more secure before winter set in. Several hours passed before he could stop and survey all he had accomplished. He was pleased with the new look of the cabin. Now, he was ready to prepare a much-needed hot meal. There was a supply of cut wood in a box by the door. Some kindling was prepared and soon he had a healthy fire crackling in the stove. Olaf got a pail of water from the lake. He placed the filled kettle and a pot on the stove to boil. Two hot bowls of porridge and several cups of strong, sweet coffee set the world right. The clear, night sky was resplendent with a full moon and twinkling stars that shone like pieces of silver waiting to be plucked from the darkness. The mournful cry of a lonely wolf floated from across the lake. Little wavelets lapped the sands of the beach with gentle slapping sounds. Olaf leaned against the doorframe, with glowing pipe in hand, and contentedly viewed the beauty that nature had put on display, as if it were a special performance for his benefit. Completely relaxed, he prepared the cabin for the night, undressed and wearily crept into his sleeping bag.

He awakened before daylight and rubbed the sleep from his eyes. As he did his morning stretch, he yawned, making a sound like a bull moose in rut. At that instance there was a scurry of little feet and protesting squeaks from his lodgers as they dashed through their get-away holes. One task for today, he decided, was to plug all cracks and holes through which the mice can gain entrance into his castle. In no time he had the stove alive with a blazing fire. The warmth oozed its way through the cabin and drove away the morning chill. He put the coffeepot on to boil. He opened a can of condensed mushroom soup and dumped this into a pot to heat. The coffeepot gurgled, announcing its readiness for a spoonful of grounds. The first cup, steaming hot and with a tantalizing aroma, was like nectar from the gods. Hot soup and crackers dispelled the hunger pangs that cramped his stomach. The left over soup was put aside for his noon lunch and the coffeepot sat on the back of the stove so as to keep the coffee hot and on the ready. A thick log was placed in the stove and the damper turned down so that the log would burn slowly and maintain some heat. The breakfast dishes were rinsed with hot water and left on the table to dry.

Olaf carefully examined the cabin to locate the holes and cracks through which the wildlife entered. There were several obvious places he found and these were solidly plugged with wedges of wood forced into the openings. The loose windowpanes were stabilized by using strips of wood tacked to the frame, inside and outside. From the inside he could see where daylight entered the cabin through chinks between some of the logs. Using a mixture of clay, twigs, pebbles and water, he prepared a thick, sticky mass and pushed this into the gaping areas and smoothed over it with a flat shingle. Inside, the mud plaster had to be smoothed as well. He examined the rest of the logs and reinforced any areas that appeared to be crumbling. Once dried, the mud plaster would seal the cabin tightly against wind, rain or snow. Olaf knew that the roof would need to be looked at because there were leaks during the storm. He constructed a crude ladder out of some small jack pine trees to allow him access to the roof. He found several places where the shingles had rotted or were blown away by the wind. With his broad axe, he shaved off the required shingles from a pine log and tacked them into place. While up on the roof, he adjusted and stabilized the stovepipe which poked through the pipe collar. Before descending, he scrutinized the whole roof to make certain that no further work was required. Satisfied, he returned to the ground and carefully surveyed his work. He was pleased with his efforts.

He went inside to enjoy a mug of coffee and a couple of hardtack biscuits. While he dined, Olaf figured that fresh, roasted fish and cooked rice would make a pleasant change to his diet. Quickly he rummaged for his rod and lures. The line was of strong linen and would take a lot of strain and successfully hold a large fish until it was landed. Before going out on the lake, Olaf started a fire in a sandpit and piled it with wood so that it would burn down into a heap of glowing embers. Over these, he would slowly roast the fish he was certain he would catch. He half filled a pot and threw in a handful of rice and placed it at the edge of the fire where it would get the benefit of the crackling flames and cook while he was out on the lake.

His canoe was stored under a pine tree that abutted the embankment on which the cabin stood. The craft was easy to handle as it gracefully glided across the still water. Olaf stopped paddling when he was about three hundred yards from the shore. Stoking his pipe, he contentedly drew the smoke and blew it out into the air where it billowed and floated away like tiny clouds. The bait was a red and white lure made from hard wood with two, triple ganged hooks attached. Within ten minutes he had caught two white fish and a large lake trout. This, he decided would be enough for a good feed.

By the time he returned to the shore and stored his canoe, the fire had formed into a domed shape pile of hot, glowing embers. The rice was gently simmering and beginning to swell as it absorbed the water. Olaf chucked in a handful of raisins and gave it a good stirring. He cleaned the fish and split them open like the pages of a book. The head and entrails were discarded along the shore for some land creatures and birds to enjoy. Now, the fire was perfect to cook the fish. Into the ground he diagonally pushed three thick, green, forked willow branches so that the forked ends extended about ten inches above the embers. The fish were placed flat, flesh side down, on the forked branches and they soon were roasted to perfection. The three fish and steaming rice with sweet raisins were, to Olaf, as tasty as any cuisine that could be eaten in an elegant, hotel dining room.

Although anxious to scout the area he would be trapping, he deliberated that it was best to complete all that needed to be done on the home front. One necessary and very important structure to be erected, with some careful planning, was the almighty outhouse. So, early the next day, with spade in hand, he searched out a suitable site, not too close to the cabin, yet not too far away either. He found the ideal spot. It was in an area about a hundred yards east of the cabin sheltered within a grove of small poplar trees. The soil was sandy and easy to dig. Within two hours, he had excavated a pit five feet deep and four feet square. He chopped down some sturdy jack pines, cleaned off the limbs and cut off the ends so that the logs were about ten feet long. A trough, three feet deep and six inches wide, was trenched around the hole with a space of two feet between them and the excavation. The logs were then stood upright, side by side, in the trench to form a palisade around the hole. On the south-facing wall he left a space to create a doorway. Earth was shovelled into the trench and tamped down solidly around the poles. Inside, he attached two sturdy frames, one on each side of the hole, to the sidewalls. Spanning the gap between the frames, he placed two logs, smoothly peeled. This arrangement afforded him a comfortable ledge to sit on. The flat roof was a series of jack-pine logs laid side by side and extended three feet beyond and over the doorway. This provided shelter from the elements. The door, itself, was a project he could put together at a later date. The warm sun was now directly above, so Olaf decided that it was time to have something to eat.

Another task he wanted to get done was to make his bunk bed more comfortable. Although he slept well enough his back muscles complained during the night and he awakened each morning feeling stiff and achy. He vowed to himself that tonight his bed would be soft and comfortable. Grasping the axe, Olaf went off into the spruce forest behind the cabin and hacked off a big pile of evergreen boughs and piled them neatly to one side. When he had amassed a large heap of branches, he carted them back to the cabin and layered them onto his bunk bed to form a springy mattress. On top of these, he laid an old piece of tarpaulin that old McGregor had used when he was in residence. The sleeping bag was stretched out over the tarp, and, immediately, he had the makings of a comfortable bed. A trial lie down proved to be the promise of comfortable sleeps ahead until the branches lost their bounce and would have to be replaced.

Against the west wall of the cabin, two rows of cured firewood were stacked the length of the cabin. Olaf surmised that this supply of fuel would see him through most of the winter, but in order not to be caught short he decided to increase the pile. This will be his project for tomorrow, but now he planned another fish and rice cookout on the beach.

After the repast, he sat at the door of his cabin and gazed out at the glass-like surface of the lake and watched the sun, resembling an inflated, orange beach-ball, sink smoothly below the horizon and then lightly tinge the under parts of the clouds a rosy pink. He recalled many moments of such tranquillity at the farm in Norway. A loon's melancholy cry floated to him from across the expansive lake. Playful trout were leaping high out of the water to snatch the insects flying low to the surface. From the forest behind the cabin, an owl's ghostly hoots penetrated the veil of darkness. A timber wolf, on the far shore, howled his plaintive cry to the moon and soon other wolves joined in the game to create a crescendo of canine music ever so pleasing to the ear. Gradually, the sounds of nature settled down, and the world around became as still and silent as a tomb. He felt a sense of calm and peace within himself. This kind of isolation and tranquillity was in itself priceless.

When Olaf retired to his bed, the night sky was clear with pinpoints of starlight and a full moon, like a huge, silver platter, shone over the lake, but during the night, the sky filled with heavy, dark clouds which blew in from the north. The rain started as a shower at first, but soon a deluge pounded the shingles with a vengeance as if demanding to be let in. He wakened earlier than usual because of the noisy reverberation on the roof and had an early breakfast. It appeared to be the kind of day which would confine him to the cabin. This, he thought, would be the day to make a batch of bread and home made baked beans as well as tidy up around the cabin. The old cooking range was fired up. The bread dough was rising in the pans, the beans were simmering in the pot and the kettle was bubbling on the back of the stove. The cabin was cosy and full of tantalizing odours that caused his mouth to salivate. The bread and beans were now baking in the oven, so he was free to work about the cabin.

He opened the door to view the dismal sight. It was pelting, and a quagmire formed all around the cabin and right down to the lakeshore. The lake level was higher than usual. He saw the canoe floating bottom up and if the lake became too high it could either float away from shore or become submerged. Neither of these options was acceptable, so Olaf had no alternative but to dress and go out to rescue his craft. The path down to the lakeshore was very wet and slippery. Twice he lost his footing and slid down on his backside. His clothing was slathered with mud, and the downpour of rain soaked him to the skin and chilled his body to the bones. He retrieved the canoe from the water with considerable effort and hauled it up to higher ground.

With that unexpected and uncomfortable chore over, he hastily retreated to the cosiness of the warm cabin and immediately stripped down and huddled close to the stove to get warm and dry off. Dry clothes and a hot cup of coffee made the world respectable again. While contemplating about all the things that needed to be done, he realized that he had lost all awareness of the days. He needed a calendar. Using the sides of a cardboard packing box, Olaf marked out rectangles to represent the months of the year. He knew the day, month and year when he left

Norway, so he was able to plan out, by mentally reviewing the number of days he had been travelling and settled at camp, that today had to be Thursday, the fourteenth of August. He decorated the wall next to his bunk with the calendar.

During the night, the rain stopped. In the morning the sky was overcast with light, grey clouds through which the sun struggled to shine. He gazed out at a peaceful scene. The lake was like glass, the trees and plants glistened with pearly raindrops, the earth was spongy, the vegetation looked renewed and bird songs filled the air. Inhaling great amounts of clean, cool air revived Olaf's senses and made him feel energetic, ready to face the day's tasks. Breakfast over with, he gathered the axe and bow-saw and headed off into the forest behind the cabin. Within a mile of his home, he came across a thick stand of spruce trees. Laboriously, he chopped down a dozen trees, limbed them and sawed them into stove-size logs. He piled them neatly so as to dry over the next few months. There were a good number of wind fallen trees that were perfectly dried and ready for the stove. He sawed and split them and then backpacked bundles of the cured wood to the cabin. The task of transporting the wood took a little over two hours. Before he called it a day, Olaf split up a huge supply of kindling, which was stored inside, close to the stove.

Olaf had to use the lake for his water supply. The Grass River was not a good alternative, as it was further away from the cabin and did not have a good access. He would have to wade out into the river before he could dip his pail. However, in front of the cabin, there was a rocky shelf that protruded out into the lake for several yards. At the end of the shelf the lake was deep, making it easy to dip the pail. During the cold winter, it would be easy to maintain a hole through the ice.

At this juncture, he was ready to turn his attentions away from the cabin and begin to explore his trapping area. So he retired earlier than usual because he planned an early start in the morning.

CHAPTER THREE
THE TRAPPING AREA

Olaf was up and about long before the sun had shown any indication of rising and made preparations for his initial excursion into his trap-line area. He had put together a simple lunch of bread and baked beans, in the form of sandwiches. He would rely on hand scooping water from a stream or pond for liquids. It was important to travel light because he wanted to cover as much ground as possible that day. To get an indication of where he would be trapping, he studied the map supplied by the Lands and Forest Branch. His area extended north along the west shore of Wekusko Lake and west along the south shore of Lake Herblet that was joined to Wekusko Lake by a shallow narrows.

With backpack on and rifle in hand, Olaf started off just as the sun was appearing above the treetops. He followed the shoreline for several miles and soon crossed an old, rutted, unused, overgrown trail. This would be one of the trails old Angus had used years back. As he progressed, Olaf blazed marks on the trees. These would keep him on target until the trail became second nature to him. Along the way he crossed several streams that emptied into the lake. On the banks of the streams, short, pointed, gnawed poplar tree stumps were proof of extensive beaver activity. There were old signs of traps and snares that Angus had set. The lake was in sight for a long ways before the trail began to veer off into the forest. His hike took him through areas of swampy pools dotted with muskrat houses and around which lush grasses, on which moose loved to feed, grew in abundance. He mentally noted that this was an excellent moose hunting area.

This appeared to be a suitable spot to stop for a snack and rest. Directly above, the sun burned like a yellow fireball. The few, wispy cirrus clouds, drifting casually above, did not provide any shelter from the direct heat of the noonday sun. Thus, he chose to sit in the shade of a spreading spruce tree and enjoyed the coolness it afforded. The stillness of the forest, beyond the pools, was awe-inspiring. The drug like atmosphere caused his heavy eyes to close and his tired body to succumb to a nap. After a short time, his conscious mind began to surface and he opened his eyes slowly. When they became focussed, he saw, directly in front of him, a cow moose staring at him. It seemed as though she was trying to determine if he posed a danger. Olaf sat frozen to the spot; his terrified heart pounded his chest wall like a jackhammer because moose have been known to kill with their razor sharp, front hooves whatever they perceived to be a threat. This thought passed through his mind. Inside his head, he was screaming for the moose to move on. After what seemed an eternity, the cow struck the ground with a front hoof, shook her head and snorted a warning before gracefully loping away. He sat very still for the longest time and gathered his wits before he brought himself to move. Once composed, he forged ahead a little further before turning back.

The trail turned east towards Herblet Lake. He came upon a small, swampy meadow surrounded by spruce, poplar and birch trees. At the far end, just inside the sheltering trees, were the remains of a line camp. It was constructed of logs and just large enough to house one person. Inside there was room for a man to lie down on a mattress of spruce boughs, a place to sit on the dirt floor and a small area to store gear. To add to the crude comfort, a small circular, stone fire pit was situated at the end furthest away from the entrance. Above this, a small portion of the roof could be removed to provide a means of exit for the smoke. No window was present. Candles would have to be used to illuminate the dingy darkness. It would take, thought Olaf, a few hours of concentrated effort to somewhat renew the shelter to its previous, liveable state. A job he would have to face in the near future. Briefly he explored the immediate area before turning back. He estimated that the shack was ten to twelve miles away from his cabin. On the way home, he scouted out a creek that tumbled slowly toward the lake. A ten minute walk brought him to a huge pond that fairly filled the area of forest opening. A beaver dam, about twenty feet long and six feet wide, extended across its end. Five beaver houses dotted the pond like warts on the back of a toad. Three beavers swam about transporting poplar branches to their lodges. A beaver, that noticed Olaf, slapped its tail on the surface and immediately disappeared. The sharp smack alerted the other two who, likewise, quickly vanished into the depths of the pond. Two beavers on the far shore scurried towards the pond and plunged in headfirst causing ripples to spread across its surface. All was still about the pond. He reckoned that this pond will provide him with a bumper crop of skins. Happily, he continued his journey and arrived home just before sunset. Tomorrow, if the weather was reasonable, Olaf planned to pack sufficient supplies and utensils to spend several days away from home.

Shafts of grey light penetrated the cabin's dark interior and faintly illuminated the main area of the room, leaving the corners in semi-darkness. Olaf leapt out of bed, anxious to be on his way. He dressed and quickly prepared his breakfast in the yellow glow of several candles. He gathered all the gear, tools and food that would be needed for at least three days. Looking about the cabin, he saw that all was in order. He closed the door snugly, but did not secure it with a lock. The code of the north was that a shelter is never locked because should a traveller happen by needing refuge he would have access, but must leave the cabin in the state he found it. That is, replenish the wood used, not abuse the supplies or steal.

The sky was overcast with dark clouds. He loped along with long strides. At this rate, he thought, he should be at his first stop in two and a half-hours. The trail was easy to hike and he noticed frequent signs of animal activity. Twice he saw bear scats in the areas where berry bushes grew in abundance. During the night, moose and deer had been moving up and down the trail. Out in the shallow water, a bull moose was feeding amongst the rushes. It slowly raised its huge antlered head and stared nonchalantly at him and then continued feeding without concern. Had this been the rut season, which it will soon be, the scenario would have probably been somewhat more disturbing. He stopped at the stream that led off to the beaver pond and chiselled several notches on the trunk of a birch tree to identify his turn-off point. Although the sky was densely packed with threatening clouds, the rain had not yet started. He reached line camp Number One near midday. Immediately he set about restoring its condition. Because the camp was in a reasonable state, it did not take long to remedy its faults. Soon, he had a cosy home away from home.

The threatening clouds were sitting low over the

treetops, a forerunner of what was to come. This spurred him onward. He wanted to get to the next camp before dark and the onslaught of the rain. The trail began to curve away from Wekusko Lake. Although it was reasonably packed and easy to follow, he still blazed his way. This would prove to be a wise decision for the future. The track made a gradual climb to a bench-land that overlooked Herblet Lake in the distance. It then snaked its way down through several draws and crossed through a small valley dotted with a small lake and interconnecting ponds. The lake was partially surrounded by a dense pine forest that hugged the far shoreline. Clusters of birch and poplar trees grew sporadically throughout the grassy meadows and around the ponds.

Beyond the valley, low, undulating hills stretched away into the distance towards the north. Beaver and muskrat houses were dotted about in all of the ponds. Around the shore, weasel tracks criss-crossed in every direction. He followed the faint trail over a rocky shelf and arrived at the edge of the forest on the east side of the lake. Here, he discovered the dilapidated remains of line camp Number Two. He saw at once that it would not be prudent to refurbish it, but better to construct a new one. A distant rumble of thunder heralded the coming of a storm. Olaf selected a dry, sheltered campsite just inside the trees. He erected a lean-to large enough to store his gear and allow him to lie down on a bed of spruce boughs. Scraping away the vegetation and dead pine needles, he made a fireplace in front of the lean-to and ringed it with rocks. Close to the entrance, he piled a great amount of tinder-dry logs. While cooking supper, fat drops of rain hurtled down and bounced off the rocks and riddled the lake's surface. Within minutes a relentless deluge obliterated the landscape. All around, lightning and thunder created a tumultuous symphony of cracking, booming and brilliant streaks of blue and white. Olaf thanked his lucky stars that he was ensconced in his simple shelter, out of reach of the downpour. Fully sated, he placed two large logs on the fire, crawled into the sleeping bag and soon was fast asleep, oblivious to nature's tirade.

The rain did not let up during the night. He awakened to a miserable, wet day. There was no sign of any respite. He resigned himself to spending the better part of the day doing very little. After eating, he sat comfortably on his bed, smoked his pipe and gazed out over the lake. Eventually, by mid-morning, the rain began to let up, and within the hour it had stopped completely. Patches of blue sky appeared through the rapidly dispersing clouds allowing the sun's shafts of comforting rays to burst through. Ghostly vapours moved upwards from the rocks and earth. Soon a thick fog hung thickly over the landscape. Olaf wasted no time in getting his tools gathered, so as to make the best of the rest of the day.

He plunged into the forest and quickly set his axe and saw to felling straight, medium sized trees suitable for building the line camp. The camp was constructed much larger than camp Number One because it would be the main camp from which he would work his trap-line. Judging from the number of beaver and rat houses he had seen, Olaf figured that he would be kept very busy. On his next trip, the sheet metal camp stove will be brought in. He worked into dusk and continued for most part of the next day. Thus, he stayed over another night.

Olaf guessed that there were two hours of daylight left, so rather than waste them, he used the time to explore the lake and ponds. Along the lakeshore there were positive signs of beaver activity. He saw where they dragged poplar limbs to the lake and floated them, through the narrows and ponds, to their lodges. Further along, the area was covered in tracks of fur bearing rodents which, he was certain, belonged to marten and muskrat. The overgrown trail skirted the edges of the ponds through boggy ground overgrown with marsh grasses and weeds. Imprinted in the sand and mud, he noticed deep tracks of moose and dainty hoof prints of deer leading down to and away from the water. Black clouds of mosquitoes and black flies swarmed all around and made it quite miserable. Since the rain stopped, the hot, humid conditions brought them out in legions, ready to attack any living creature, big or small. To protect himself, Olaf slathered mud onto his face, neck, arms and hands. When the mud dried, it formed a protective barrier against the wicked, blood sucking hordes. Several hundred yards beyond the end of the pond, the trail swung sharply away, in a westerly direction, and disappeared into the dense forest. He hiked the trail for ten minutes. Old, barely discernable, blazes scarred the tree trunks, approximately every fifty yards. He was certain that the trail would lead him back to his home cabin. He would take this route in anticipation that it would come out at his place. On the way back to the lean-to, three mule deer were grazing in the meadow by the lake. When they espied him, they hurriedly bounded across the land as if their legs were spring loaded. He mused that some roasted deer meat would be heavenly to sink his teeth into. When he gets back to the cabin, he knew that a hunt for fresh meat was in order.

The sun was barely up when he broke camp, hiked across the meadow and headed into the forest. The morning air was pleasantly cool. The pesky bugs were out to greet him and partake in a bloody feast, but within the confines of the evergreen forest, the air was much cooler and the insect numbers thinned out considerably. It was an enjoyable hike through the trees. Olaf found evidence of old wires, attached to trees and bushes, that trapper Angus had used to snare rabbits and wild cats. A rusty wolf trap, anchored to a tree by a chain, lay in the bush off the trail. The remnant of an animal's foot was clasped in the jaws of the sprung trap. Sometimes, frightened, desperate animals will chew off their foot to escape the frightening captor. Gradually the path began an ascent to a bench land. On top, He discovered a well used animal track that led him to a lake that had several small streams flowing into it. In the shallows, at the end of the lake, several muskrat domes broke the surface like miniature hills. There were no signs of beaver habitation, but, as well as muskrat, there were tracks of marten and weasel. Halfway around the lake, he discovered line camp Number Three. It was somewhat larger than Number One and in better condition. It would not take him long to clean it out and do some minor repairs to the roof. The warm sun was nearing high noon.

Olaf looked up from his work and watched a black bear saunter along the shore. With a ponderous gait, it turned and headed towards him. A hundred yards from him the beast stopped and methodically sniffed the air. Uncertain as to what its senses were relaying to it, the bear rose on his hind legs for a better look. Suddenly, the bear reacted and, from his large gaping mouth, there erupted a ferocious growl that rumbled up from the depths of his chest. Olaf did not know if the bear would charge with the intent to do him harm, or just put up a false front to intimidate him. He did not have long to wait. The bear dropped his front legs to the ground and, with what seemed to be the force and speed of an express train, charged directly towards him, snarling through gnashing teeth and flinging saliva in every direction. The enraged animal had to clamber up a steep, rocky incline, thus slowing him down.

Olaf briefly relived the terrifying moment when a crazed bull, on his father's farm two years ago, had charged directly at him. At the very last moment, he adroitly stepped aside and forcefully knocked it on the skull with the heavy iron bar he was carrying for protection. This stunned the bull and brought it to its knees, allowing him sufficient time to quickly climb the fence to safety. His father immediately had the animal destroyed to prevent harm or possible death to a member of the family. He was now in the same kind of dangerous predicament. Olaf gripped the handle of the heavy, double bladed axe and intently watched the fearless beast rushing at him. Fear was in his heart, but never the less he stood his ground. Every muscle throughout his body was taut, ready for what was ahead, and as nervous as he felt, Olaf kept his head clear of everything but the ever nearing, deadly mass of fury.

The enraged bear charged blindly at its intended victim but Olaf sidestepped his foe with the agility of a bullfighter. As it passed close to his body, he mustered every ounce of strength within his body and brought the axe down heavily onto the animal's head, splitting it wide open. The beast momentarily stumbled, bawled in pain and then collapsed into a lifeless heap. The axe bit deeply into its brain, killing it instantly. Olaf stood dumbfounded, staring at the black mass lying before him. Shock set in and he began to tremble. He slowly sunk to the ground and sobbed uncontrollably. It was then that the realization of what could have happened took over his mind. He could have been killed. On two occasions now, he had faced situations that brought him close to death. Gradually, he returned to a normal state of mind and body.

He looked around him. Blood was splattered on the trees, bushes, his clothing and body. Down at the lake he stripped off his clothing and gave them a thorough rinsing and washed himself. In the heat of the sun, his body and clothing would soon dry. Olaf ate his lunch in his birthday suit. By the time he finished eating, his clothes were sufficiently dry to wear.

He strolled over to view the carcass which, in all appearance, looked like a black, crumpled, fur robe that had been carelessly dropped to the forest floor. Olaf decided to skin the animal and get rid of the carcass by dragging it into the woods for the carnivorous creatures to feast upon. He had never skinned a bear, but he was not too concerned about how well he was doing the task because it would just be a covering for his bunk. The bear's body showed signs of previous wounds that had festered and probably had filled his system with poison.

He was very skinny and appeared to be malnourished. This would account for his crankiness and aggression. Using a rope he dragged the carcass well into the woods away from his camp. He then scraped away the fat and loose tissue from the hide. It was a messy and laborious chore. When finished, he draped the hide over a log close to the fire in order to dry somewhat before he toted it home. After supper, Olaf sat by the fire and reminisced about the day's events. He grinned and guffawed and loudly proclaimed this camp to be "Dead Bear Camp". The black sky was like a blanket over the landscape and stars twinkled like icy blue gems. Olaf went to his bed and just before drifting off, he heard a wolf pack, deep in the woods, snarling and arguing over the bear carcass.

Olaf knew that the day was going to be very hot because the sky was cloudless and the sun was rising above the horizon like a fireball, beaming its rays onto the land below. After breakfast, he packed his gear and rolled up the bear robe. Before leaving, Olaf took a walk into the forest to where he left the bear's body. There was very little of it left. The flesh eaters, it appeared, had a veritable banquet. He hoisted the pack and bearskin onto his back and headed home. The hike was uneventful. He blazed some trees and mentally filed away important aspects of this part of the loop. He crossed many little streams that lazily flowed through the forest on their way to the lake. Animal signs were numerous, which indicated a prolific trapping area.

It was early in the afternoon when Olaf arrived at his cabin. It was a sight for sore eyes. He unloaded at the door and entered the dim cabin. Everything appeared to be as he had left it, except for a piece of paper lying on the table. He picked it up and saw that it was a note, scrawled in large, poorly shaped letters. He read that the author had passed by and used the cabin for a night and hoped to see him on his way through another time. It was signed Bert Bates. Olaf was pleased to know that there was another human in the area and looked forward to a possible visit, hopefully soon. After putting away all the gear, He unrolled the bearskin and laid it out on the ground. With soapy water and a rough stone, he cleaned off the remaining pieces of fat, meat and blood and then rinsed the hide with several pails of clean water. Now, he felt that his body needed some cleansing, and what better way to do it other than plunging into the lake. The chill of the water initially shocked him but the more he frolicked about, the warmer it began to feel. He soaped his body and rinsed off by submerging like a loon. Olaf felt highly revitalized and the long hot, sweaty hike home was now a thing in the past. This was a good time to get some laundry done, so he dunked and soaped his clothing and then pounded them on the rock to loosen the grime. A good sloshing up and down in the water rinsed the soapy apparel clean. His drying rack was a large flat, rock on which he spread his clothing in the warmth of the sun.

For his supper, he caught several large trout which he roasted over the glowing coals and supplemented them with bannock, unleavened bread cooked in a frying pan, and beans. Darkness had fallen and he now felt the strain of the physical and emotional output over the past few days. It was time to go to bed, but first he rolled up the bearskin and placed the bundle inside the cabin. Olaf crawled into his sleeping bag and let out a contented sigh of relief. Momentarily, he felt a pang of homesickness. How nice it would be to see and talk to his family. As he was drifting off, he mumbled that he would write them a long letter

CHAPTER FOUR
NEIGHBOURS

Olaf's food supplies needed to be replenished so he planned a few days of fishing and hunting. To preserve the fresh food, he erected a drying stage on which the fish and strips of meat could be dried for future use. In a short space of time he had built the stage using sturdy, birch saplings. After the mid-day meal, he spent the afternoon fishing. He caught eight fat, firm trout and eleven, large white fish. Cleaning and preparing the fish was a messy chore. He gutted them, removed their heads and rinsed their bodies in the lake. Next, he cut along the backbone to the base of the tail, which left the two halves joined at the tail. These he hung, like two pegged socks, over the crosspieces above a slow, smouldering fire of green, pine chips placed on hot coals.

As Olaf set off to hunt, the sun was poking its rim above the tree tops and the lake was beginning to ripple slightly due to a soft, warm breeze that was filtering in from the southeast. The canoe glided along swiftly and silently as he scouted along the shoreline looking for ungulates. The early morning hours are when the animals come to drink after a night of resting. The Lee Enfield rifle was close at hand, ready for action at the first sign of game. He enjoyed the tranquillity and marvelled at the scenery. The sun had crept higher and he felt its pleasant warmth through his flannel shirt. The foliage was taking on the tinges of the varying fall colours. There was a vibrant quality to the air. Suddenly, he was jolted from his day dreaming, because there, in front of him, stood a regal, six-point mule deer. It was standing on a grassy point of land that jutted out into the lake. The buck was not aware of the canoe sliding ghost like towards him. The animal's eyes were transfixed on a flock of geese settling down on the far side of the lake.

Olaf stopped paddling and carefully reached for the rifle. He raised it to his shoulder and lined it up at a point where the deer's heart would be. The loud explosion shattered the stillness of the land. The newly landed geese catapulted into the air, complaining loudly at the disturbance. The deer collapsed as the bullet ripped into his body. Quickly he propelled the craft to the shore and beached it. The animal he had killed was sleek and fat. As he gazed at it, he felt somewhat sad about taking the life of such a beautiful creature. However, he thought to himself, this was the law of the jungle. With his sharp hunting knife, he gutted the animal and removed its intestines. He kept the heart and liver aside to be taken home with the carcass. With considerable physical effort, he dragged the body to the canoe and carefully loaded it into the centre so as to maintain stability while paddling. It was late in the afternoon when the cabin was sighted.

He placed the liver and heart into a bucket of cold water. Then with a rope tied around the base of the antlers, the buck was dragged up the bank. At the side of the cabin stood a lofty, sturdy birch tree with long limbs extending well away from its trunk. Over one of the higher limbs Olaf threw a long rope with which he was able to hoist the animal's body well above the ground and secure it safely out of the reach of marauding animals. Tomorrow he will construct a storage box and encase it with screening.

After thoroughly rinsing the liver and heart, Olaf left the heart in a bucket of salted water and placed it on the roof where the cold night air would refrigerate it and keep it out of reach of animals. The day's activities had made him ravenous. He set about preparing his main meal of fried liver, rice and bannock. The fire in the stove crackled as it radiated a pleasant warmth throughout the cabin. The rice was put on to boil and the bannock dough was slapped together and moulded into flat cakes and placed in the oven. He sliced the liver into generous portions and sprinkled them with seasoned flour. The cast iron pan was liberally loaded with lard. Soon the slices of liver were set gently into the hot grease where they sizzled and cooked to perfection. He attacked his meal with great gusto and it was not long before his appetite was sated. There was enough left for a meal the next day.

Before turning in for the night, he went and checked out the hanging buck and the heart on the roof. There was a tingling chill in the night air and he was certain that there would be a light frost by morning. The stars twinkled like jewels and the light of the full moon reflected brightly from the surface of the still lake. A wolf pack was in chorus on the far side of the lake, probably in full chase of some hapless deer or moose. With a long stretch and a loud yawn, Olaf snuggled down contentedly into his sleeping bag. Sleep stealthily took command and it was not long before snorts and low buzzing sounds permeated the stillness of the dark cabin.

He constructed a sturdy, screened drying box. Skinning and quartering the deer carcass was easy for him because, on the home farm, he did this with butchered cows. He cut some of the meat into thin, narrow strips and hung them over the drying stage to make jerky - strips of hard, dried meat that do not need refrigerating and could be carried easily whilst on the trap lines. The quartered sections, along with the ribs and loin, were hung inside the box and suspended from a high limb. The netting would keep the flies from sullying the meat with maggots and the cool breezes would dry the outer surface to form a protective crust, thus preserving its freshness. The antlers were sawed off to be placed over the entrance door. The inner part of the hide was scraped clean and hung out to dry. When it was completely dried, it would be rolled up and placed next to the bear hide. The unusable parts of the carcass were dumped in the woods, well away from his cabin.

Prior to his evening meal, he settled himself down to write a long letter to his family. There was so much to write about since he left the shores of Norway. When he put the pencil to paper, a steady flow of words spread rapidly across the pages. Excited about sharing his experiences, Olaf wrote steadily for an hour. The sun was hastily sliding out of sight and the dusky light forced him to fire up the lamps before he could read over what he had written. Well pleased with having finished the missive, he turned his attention to his supper. He cooked up a large batch of biscuits that would do for supper and over the next few days. Canned beans, biscuits and roast heart were heartily feasted upon. A couple of mugs of strong, sweet tea put a pleasant closure to the events of the day just before bedtime.

Olaf awakened to a landscape swathed in hoarfrost. The coldness of the frosty air caused his breath to condense into miniature, billowy clouds. Today, he had in mind to explore Herblet Lake and area. The conditions were ideal. Cotton like clouds were interspersed throughout an azure sky and a slight breeze wafted across the water, creating wavelets. After breakfast, he loaded his gear, rifle and food into the canoe. A quick inspection around the outside of the cabin revealed that there were visitors during the night. Under his meat cache were signs of canine prints in the dirt all around the tree. A hungry wolf pack had explored ways to relieve him of his stores, but went away disappointed. The sleek canoe flitted across the water effortlessly. Its bow sliced into the water and formed a wake that widened as the craft moved ahead. The hardwood trees were beginning to lose their summer green and take on the first trace of fall reds and yellows. In the distance, on the far shore, a wide sandy beech stretched out into the lake. Several small streams emptied themselves noisily into the lake as they tumbled over the multitude of rocks that littered their beds.

Olaf explored every bay and inlet along the shore. Cranberries were in abundance in the shallows. He made a mental note to gather a supply at a later date to add some spice to his winter menu. Large fish leapt from the water to capture low flying insects. Just before noon he entered the narrows that led into Herblet Lake. The central channel appeared to be deep and the shore on each side was crowded with marsh grass and reeds. Noisy ducks floated about mindless of his presence and a variety of small water birds darted back and forth above him. At the end of the channel, he entered Herblet Lake, which was not as large as Lake Wekusko. He guessed that it would be about fifteen miles long and four miles wide.

Most of the west shore was rocky and the land was low lying with scattered stunted pines. In the clear water, huge trout were lazily swimming under the canoe. He entered a shallow bay that extended inland several hundred yards. He landed the canoe and had his midday snack. After eating, he scanned the lay of the land before him. Because of the lowness and lack of vegetation, this area would not be a good trapping area. Further back, the larger spruce, pine and birch trees dominated the higher bench-lands.

Proceeding further up the lake, Olaf came to a wide arm that extended westwards for a considerable distance. Olaf steered the craft up the arm. He saw that the trees were increasing in size and growing closer to the water's edge. Twenty minutes had passed before he decided to turn back, as it was getting late and he did not relish travelling in the dark. As he was about to turn, he saw smoke billowing above the treetops. This was not the smoke from a forest fire, but that of a campfire or a chimney. This was a surprise, because, as far as he knew there were no other humans in this area. He continued paddling. It was not long before he came to a small bay, and, to his great surprise, he saw a tidy log cabin in a clearing surrounded by the forest. On the beach two overturned canoes lay side by side. In front of the cabin a little girl was playing with a small dog and a woman was scrubbing clothing in a round metal tub. A man was chopping wood and piling it along the cabin wall. As he approached the beach, a huge dog bolted towards him, barking its head off. This alerted the people and they simultaneously looked up towards him. The child ran and hid behind her mother. The man put aside his axe and casually approached the beach to greet him. The dog stopped barking when the master came near. Olaf beached his craft and stepped out to meet the stranger.

Olaf extended his hand and introduced himself. The man grasped it firmly and stated that he was William Watson and introduced his wife, Betty and ten-year-old daughter, Josie. The Watsons were excited and pleased to have a visitor. Olaf learned that William was a trapper from the United States. He had brought his family to this area four years ago and is running a trap-line north of Finger Bay. They sold the farm and assets in Idaho and came north to Manitoba, hoping to get rich from trapping. Thus far, his efforts have only provided a reasonable living. They had known old Angus, a fine old fellow. Betty had been a teacher back home and she now schools Josie. The huge, part husky, part shepherd bitch was Lady who had given birth to the three small dogs who were romping about like children. In turn, Olaf told them about himself.

Betty insisted that he join them for supper and, due to the lateness of the day, he was also invited to spend the night. Supper consisted of a tasty stew of moose meat, wild onions and home grown potatoes in thick gravy, baked beans and thick slabs of homemade bread. Dessert was wild berry pie smothered in a creamy vanilla-sauce. The rest of the evening was passed in conversation over cups of tea. It was well into the night when all were talked out and ready for bed. Josie had been put to bed hours earlier. Olaf bedded down on a bear rug in front of the stove along side of Lady and her three, furry off-springs.

The household wakened to a morning steeped in a steady, chilly downpour. Thus, Olaf remained another day and night. William was able to impart much knowledge about trapping to Olaf. He showed him the types of traps and snares used and explained how to best set them and where. Olaf was reminded that there was a trading post at the south end of Wekusko Lake at Hall's Landing. The day passed quickly and by late evening the rain had stopped. Olaf left early the next day. As a parting gift, William gave Olaf a male dog from Lady's litter. He claimed that Olaf would find the dog to be of great service when it grows larger and stronger. With promises of seeing each other again, Olaf left his new friends standing on the shore, waving and shouting their goodbyes.

The conditions for travelling were excellent. The air was warm, the water surface was like a mirror and the sky was a brilliant blue. The young dog, silver grey, with streaks of brown and black, and a large head with upright pointed ears, sat nonchalantly in the bow of the canoe, looking around like a tourist on an organized tour. Olaf was pleased to have acquired the animal and immediately became attached to it. The dog, he felt, was intelligent and would be easy to train. Each time he spoke to it, the creature reacted by wagging his tail and cocking his head as if questioning what he said. He racked his brain to come up with a name for his pet and companion. Suddenly, it came to him. He would call him Thor, the Norse mythological god of thunder and the son of Odin. He called out Thor and the dog swivelled his head around and looked at him as if he understood that it was his name.

After passing through the narrows to Wekusko Lake, Olaf landed the craft on a small sandy beach and enjoyed moose meat sandwiches prepared by Betty. Thor was happy to get out and scamper around and sniffle at everything new to him. When it came time to depart, Olaf called the dog, who came immediately, and pointed to the canoe and told him to get in. Thor did as he was commanded. They stopped at the cranberry patch and examined the berries for their state of readiness. It would be another two to three weeks, he figured, before they would be ready for harvesting. It seemed that in no time he saw his cabin in the distance. Coming back to his rustic home always gave him a feeling of joy and contentment. As soon as the canoe touched land, Thor hopped out and scrambled about to explore his new home. Olaf was so pleased to have him. Now he can have conversations with a living form rather than talk to himself. All was in order with the cabin and it did not take long to unload and put things away. He and Thor enjoyed a hearty meal of deer steak and rice. The evening passed quickly and, at bedtime, Olaf crawled into his sleeping bag and Thor curled up on a mat at the side of the bunk. What new adventures lay ahead wondered Olaf, as he drifted off to sleep.

It was when the sun was at its zenith and Olaf was working outside, his ears picked up a faint droning sound. Shielding his eyes from the sun, he scanned the sky to the north. In the distance, he saw a dark speck rapidly approaching. He recognized Jim Barnes' plane as he watched it come down and the floats gently kiss the smooth surface. As the pontoons settled snugly into the water, Jim turned the craft toward the shore and gunned the motor before shutting it down. The plane glided up to the landing like a graceful swan. The men enthusiastically greeted each other. Olaf learned that Jim was in the area because he had to fly some prospectors further north, so he decided to stop by on the way back. Jim unloaded a crate containing magazines, potatoes, onions, carrots, apples, smokes, jam, a short wave battery operated radio and a letter from his friend, Stefan. The two men chatted happily as they carried the goods up to the cabin. An hour and a half passed quickly as they crammed in as much news as possible over cups of coffee and yeast biscuits. Jim said that he would be flying in the area once more just before freeze-up to deliver winter supplies to the prospectors and on the way back he will drop down and deliver any supplies he may need. Olaf was happy to make out a shopping list. Jim was given a blank cheque to cover the costs of the new order and the goods brought in during this trip. He asked Jim if he would mail the letter to his family. Thor took to Jim like a duck to water and accepted him as a member of the family. The plane pulled away from the shore with ease and was soon airborne.

Olaf packed away the supplies and got the radio operational. Now he would have communication from the outside. Stefan's letter was left to the last as he wanted to digest the contents at his leisure. To his dismay, he read that Stefan was leaving Canada to return home to Norway as his father had passed away and his mother needed him to run the family farm because there were no siblings to take over. His younger brother died of meningitis at an early age. Stefan asked Olaf to write to him. He felt sad that his friend was not able to pursue his dream.

With fresh vegetables and choice cuts of deer meat, Olaf prepared a tasty stew for his supper. All the ingredients were put on to boil and then gently simmered for several hours. Fresh baked yeast biscuits were in order to sop up the gravy and also to be slathered with jam for dessert.

The evening sky looked promising for the next day. A full moon illuminated the landscape like a flood-lamp and the Milky Way stretched across the night sky like a handful of diamonds carelessly flung over the surface of a black tablecloth. In the northern sky the aurora borealis billowed like multicoloured curtains blowing in a gentle breeze. The frosty, chill of the night air caused an involuntary shiver to permeate his body. It would not be long before the first signs of winter will appear, heralding the season of the big sleep. Olaf wanted to prepare the line camps for the trapping season before this occurred.

CHAPTER FIVE
BERT BATES

During the warm, hazy Indian Summer days and frosty nights of October, the deciduous trees became resplendent in their full colours of red, orange, yellow and rust. A morning breeze gently rattled the leaves, creating a sound as if a thousand sprites were lightly dancing across sheets of crumpled newspaper. Olaf stood in the doorway and viewed the entire landscape and wondered in awe at the splendour of nature. The lake reflected the magnificent colours from its glass like surface. Thor appeared to appreciate the view as much as he did. His tiny tail wagged rapidly and his pink tongue lolled out one side of his smiling mouth.

Morning was well into the day by the time Olaf had gathered all his gear for the line camps. He decided to outfit Dead Bear Camp first as it was the furthest away and would require an overnight stay. The traps and snares were assembled into three groups, one for each camp. Dead Bear Camp would need the bulk of the gear, because its area was the largest to be worked. He would use the canoe to transport his paraphernalia to the narrows at the end of the lake. From there, he would break trail in a north westerly line and figured he should come out reasonably close to the camp. By not using the regular route, his travel time was shortened considerably. With the dog and gear loaded, Olaf paddled the canoe effortlessly across the still water. He travelled for about an hour when he steered the craft towards the shore and beached it near the mouth of a shallow stream. Thor quickly jumped from the canoe and happily scurried about to explore the new terrain. To his great surprise, he had accidentally flushed a bevy of partridge. After a hasty snack of some hardtack and cool water from the stream, Olaf loaded up, and with compass in hand, headed off into the wilderness in the direction of Dead Bear Camp.

His direct bearing was north by west, towards the rolling hills south of Herblet Lake. Along the way he blazed a route through the dense woods. Occasionally he was forced to chop away some heavy undergrowth and fallen trees. To his surprise and delight, after approximately two hours, they hit the trail that led to Dead Bear Camp. In thirty minutes they were at the door of the shack. There were signs of someone having been at the site recently. He saw the remains of a campfire, trampled grass and the door was ajar, otherwise all else was in order. It appeared, from the amount of disruption to the grass area, that several people had been in attendance.

He was perplexed and wondered who the visitors might have been. Nevertheless, he thought, their identity may be revealed at a later date. He stashed his traps in the far corner, away from the door, and then set about to prepare a supply of firewood. The sun had descended below the treetops and the evening air chilled rapidly. Olaf decided that now would be a good time to test the shelter. A cheerful fire provided warmth and light. After his meal, he fired up the pipe, sat comfortably on the bare floor with his back against the wall and enjoyed the solitude of his surroundings. In all he was very pleased with how well all worked out in the shelter. Winter will provide no hardship for them inside this camp. Prior to bedding down, they went outside to do their toilet duties. The night air was frosty and a full moon shone brilliantly over the landscape. He snuggled into the cosy comfort of his sleeping bag and Thor curled up into a round bundle at the foot. Soon the silence was disturbed with loud, snores that only deep sleep could bring.

When Olaf let Thor out for his morning functions, the entire landscape was a vista of pure whiteness due to a heavy, hard frost. Thor, at first, displayed a cautious wonderment at this new phenomena and viewed it with suspicion. However, when he became accustomed to the situation, he happily frolicked through the cold vegetation.

After breakfast, Olaf tidied the area around the

camp and hung his traps inside the shelter. With the camp secured, they set out on their homeward journey. The return trip to the lake took longer than coming as more clearing of the trail had to be done, and, as well, he scouted the area for signs of mink, marten and fisher. By noon they reached the shore.

A check of the cranberries found that they were ready for harvesting. After two hours, Olaf estimated that there were at least thirty pounds collected in the bottom of the canoe. These he would wash thoroughly and spread out on a ground sheet to dry in the sun. It was dusk when they arrived home. Thor ran around giving the place his inspection and returned wagging his tail, as if declaring all was in order. That evening, before retiring, Olaf gave himself the pleasure of listening to the radio. He now did not feel shut off from the rest of the world. He thought that, some day, it would be ideal to have a two-way communication system, but at this juncture he could not afford such a luxury.

Olaf was in the midst of preparing a breakfast of fried deer steak and baked beans. The coffeepot was steaming at the back of the stove and slices of homemade bread were browning in the oven. Outside, Thor was incessantly barking and sounded quite agitated so he strode to the door and looked out. The dog was standing on the shore looking at something out on the lake. He closely scanned the surface and espied a canoe in the distance coming towards his landing. He called the animal to him and they stood motionless watching the approaching craft. As the craft came nearer, Thor emitted throaty growls.

The visitor adroitly beached the canoe. When he stepped out on to the shore, Olaf could not help notice the hugeness of this man. He took long, determined strides towards the cabin and his long arms swung easily from his shoulders. His shoulders were broad and his chest bulged, causing his shirt to stretch tightly around him. The man's bulk and walk portrayed confidence as well as arrogance. As he neared the cabin, the visitor loudly introduced himself as Bert Bates, the one who had previously left Olaf a note. Olaf greeted him and introduced himself and the dog. He invited the visitor to share breakfast. Bert quickly accepted, stating that he had not eaten since the evening before, as his supplies had run out. Thor was not entirely resigned to accepting this person or his intrusion. He stayed out of reach and did not offer any friendly, puppy attention to him.

During breakfast, the men indulged in small talk about trapping and the country around. Bert said he trapped in an area at the north East End of Herblet Lake a little ways up Cutter Creek. He was on his way to the trading post at Hall's Landing to fetch in some winter supplies. Bert said he saw smoke over the cabin and knew that someone was at home, so he swung over to meet the occupant. Olaf asked him if he had been up to Dead Bear

Camp recently and used the site. Bert said that he has never been up in that part of the country and suggested that it could have been some Cree Indians from the Fox Lake Reserve north of Herblet Lake. They apparently travelled about the country freely.

Several hours had passed when Bert arose and thanked Olaf for his hospitality and stated that he must be on his way, as there were many miles ahead of him to paddle. Olaf packed a lunch for Bert and wished him well on his journey. As he watched the visitor make his way across the lake, Olaf felt uneasy about him and a shiver ran down his spine. He sensed that Bert was a man who needed to be watched and not to be trusted. He muttered to himself that he hoped to never see him again, but little did he know how much Bert was to impact on his life.

It was too late in the day for him to make a trip to line camp Number One, so he resigned himself to doing chores around the camp. Now was a good time to make the door for the latrine. With winter approaching, he would need some protection from the elements while occupying the throne. Upon completion, Olaf stood and admired his handy work. After a hasty lunch, with axe and bow saw in hand, he hiked into the forest to where he had stock piled logs for his stove. He felled and sawed several trees and piled the logs in the shelter of several pine trees to cure for future use. As evening approached he stopped work. After supper he wrote a long letter to his friend Stefan.

He expressed his sorrow about Stefan's predicament and also brought him up to date about himself.

Within a period of three days Olaf was able to outfit the two line camps in readiness for the season. On his homeward journey from camp Number Two, he was passing through the area in which he first encountered the female moose. Olaf stopped dead in his tracks when the deafening roar of a rifle shot echoed throughout the forest. Olaf was mystified, as he believed he was the only person in the vicinity. Cautiously, he advanced along the trail in the direction from which the shot came. He entered a low, swampy area where in the future he planned to set traps. Just to the right, off the trail, he heard muffled, gutteral voices. Leaving the trail he quietly approached the spot from where the talking came and entered a clearing where he saw two people bent over a gutted bull moose. From the way they were attired, in buckskin trousers and shirt, he figured that they must be Cree Indians from the Fox Lake Reserve. Utter surprise registered upon the Indians' faces when they first noticed him standing off to one side. In broken English they asked who he was and what he was doing in this region. When Olaf explained who he was and what he was doing here, they relaxed and became friendlier. The Indians said that they were out hunting for the reserve on Fox Lake about twenty miles from here. Thor did not know what to make of these strangers, so he stayed very close to Olaf's legs. The natives gave him a gift of moose meat and an open invitation to visit the reserve. Likewise, an invitation was extended to them and others in their tribe to visit him whenever they were in the area. Olaf did not feel threatened with the Crees coming into his territory to hunt, but he hoped they would not intrude onto his trapping zone. That night, Thor and Olaf enjoyed a tasty feast of tender moose steak, rice and bannock. As he sat and mulled over the day's events, tiredness began to pervade his whole being, forcing him to call it a day. Besides, tomorrow they have to be away early to bag either a deer or moose to replenish the dwindling supply of venison.

An early morning mist was rising eerily from the surface of the lake as Olaf quietly guided the canoe along the shore. The thickness of the fog muffled all sounds, so he had to listen intently for any indication of animal movement. Thor, sitting so still on the prow of the boat, looked like a ceramic dog. He seemed to sense the urgency and thrill of stalking unseen prey. Olaf would paddle a few casual strokes and then let the canoe drift while he listened. The dog was beginning to fidget as though he sensed something through the fog. He stopped paddling and strained his ears. The muted sounds of dripping water and slow, sloshing movements riveted Olaf's attention. These were an indication that a moose was having its morning feed of succulent plants growing in the water. He gently and silently steered the craft towards the direction of the sounds. Through the mist, he made out the hazy shape of a moose close to the shore. It was oblivious of the intruders entering his area. As the canoe pierced through the dense gloom, the beast's body loomed clearly into view. It had its head under water, so it was not aware of the approaching peril. Olaf reached for the rifle and cautiously released the safety, raised it to his shoulder and targeted the area just behind the ear for a clean kill. Thor, who could not contain his excitement any further, let out a low growl just as the moose lifted its head from the water.

Alerted by the sound, it turned, and looked directly at the boat and its occupants. This action spoiled Olaf's aim, so he could not get off the shot he wanted. The frightened animal quickly turned as if on a pivot and effortlessly bounded for the shore. Thor was now barking as if possessed which spurred the moose to accelerate his escape as he broke from the water. It bounded straight for the trees, but for some reason, only known to the beast, it veered sharply to the right and ran parallel to the shore. This gave Olaf an excellent opportunity for a broadside shot. The animal stumbled, gained its footing and limped into the woods. Olaf, realising that he had wounded the animal, hurriedly beached the canoe and gave pursuit with Thor running ahead leading him in the direction to the wounded animal. It was an easy trail to follow as the animal had bled profusely and its blood had spattered onto the trees and bushes. He could hear Thor off to the left harassing the moose, so it seemed apparent that it had stopped to fight the dog. It was easy to find them. It took one well directed shot to put the moose out of its misery.

Olaf wiped the sweat from his face. He saw that the first shot hit just behind the right front shoulder. It ran a short distance before having to stop due to the excessive loss of blood. It was a young animal that, he estimated, weighed about seven hundred pounds. Thor sniffed around the body and appeared pleased with himself for the part he played in this drama. It took a couple of hours to skin and quarter the carcass. Olaf packed the hind and front quarters, heart and liver to the canoe and covered them with the hide. The rest of the body was left to the creatures of the forest to feed upon. Dusk was upon them by the time he had brought the meat home and hung it up in the drying box, but not before slicing off several thick steaks for their evening meal. The heart and liver were prepared and stored on the roof.

In the early morning Olaf looked out onto a landscape that was covered in thick frost. The lake had a skin of thin ice protruding several yards from the shore. A change in the season was imminent. He decided that it was time to visit the Watson's before freeze-up set in. From the drying box he took out a hindquarter and filled a bucket with cranberries to take to the Watsons.

Three hours of steady paddling brought him to Watsons' place. White smoke was billowing from the chimney, a welcome sight to the weary travellers. A chorus of barking and excited yelps alerted the occupants who came tumbling out of the cabin en masse. Surprised delight registered on their faces when they saw who it was. The dogs were equally happy to be reunited with Thor who frolicked about crazily with his family. The rest of the day was spent in joyous feasting and exchange of news and happenings. Olaf made ready to leave so that he and Thor would reach home before darkness fell. Betty and William invited him to come and stay several days over Christmas. Olaf gladly accepted. With a warm feeling in his heart, he propelled the canoe away from the landing, and, with a final wave, slowly disappeared into the distance.

CHAPTER SIX
HUDSON'S BAY POST

October blended into November and the autumn breezes had greedily plucked the dry leaves from the deciduous trees, leaving the landscape bare of colour other than the green of the conifer trees. Periodically, icy blasts of air would filter down from the north, warning that winter was approaching. For some time, Olaf had in mind to take a trip down to the Hudson Bay Trading Post at Hall's Landing at the south end of the lake. He wanted to make arrangements to sell his furs and to purchase supplies. The trip, he estimated would take three days, there and back, so he assembled his gear and food accordingly. As they paddled from the icy shore, the early morning air enveloped them in a shroud of misty coldness. An hour of hard paddling had passed before the sun slid into view and provided some warmth. Olaf steered his course close to the west shore because the lake, as he remembered from the flight over it, narrowed considerably at the south end and thus would be a shorter crossing to the east shore and the Landing. Close to the shore they disturbed an angry bull moose which boldly charged down to the water's edge, snorted viciously and made threatening gestures. Several cows were quietly grazing in the tall grasses, ignoring this display of ownership over them. Olaf realized that it was the rutting season and decided it would be wise to steer wide of him.

The sun was over head when they entered a narrow bay and beached the canoe onto a white, sandy shore. Here, they would rest a while and have a bite to eat. As he glanced around, Olaf spotted a derelict log cabin nestled amongst the pines. The naked windows on each side of the dangling door stared hauntingly over the lake. The crumbling, stone chimney thrust itself crazily above what remained of the roof. The weathered, log walls stood askew on their foundations. A suffocating growth of vegetation and small bushes surrounded it as if holding it to siege. The abandoned cabin looked pathetic in its state of decay, a far cry from what it must have been when first built. He made his way up to the ancient, grey shell along a densely, overgrown path. He gently pushed the door, causing it to fall to the dusty, dirt floor. It took a few moments for his eyes to adjust to the dimness. Daylight entering through the windows, doorway, holes in the roof and empty spaces between the logs provided enough illumination to easily scan the small room. The crude furnishings, made of logs, were in various stages of collapse and deterioration. The table and one chair stood lob-sided, ready to fall over with the least provocation. In the far corner there was a wide shelf, which must have been the bed, and it looked reasonably sound. Along one wall, two shelves, barely attached, held several rusty tin containers that stood like old soldiers at attention. There was no cook stove, but at one end of the room there was a rock fireplace, the source of heat and means of cooking. A collapsed wood-box carelessly spilled its contents of very old, dry logs onto the floor. Olaf thought, compared to this hovel, his cabin was a palace.

A shaft of light brought his attention to some faint carving on the log over the door. He was able to decipher the words "Pierre Deboise, July, 1885". There was nothing to indicate whether Pierre was a trapper or a prospector. Olaf wondered about the kind of meagre and difficult existence Deboise must have suffered thirty-five years ago. He scouted around the outside. Nature was reclaiming its own with overgrown grasses, weeds and trees, that choked out any semblance of the human habitation that once had prevailed here. Because his rest and lunch time were consumed in exploring the cabin, Olaf had to be on his way immediately, and had to satisfy his hunger by munching on hard-tack and jerky while paddling. After what seemed endless hours of paddling, he saw that the lake was beginning to narrow and the shoreline was thick with reeds that extended into the lake. At the far end he saw the outlines of a large, white building, the Hudson's Bay trademark in the north. Long before he neared the Landing, Olaf heard dogs barking and howling.

As they neared the beach, several native children and camp dogs were there to greet them. Strangers were not something new to them, so they approached quite boldly and bombarded Olaf with questions in broken English. Thor was not sure of how to accept these precocious children, so he hung back timidly. Olaf tolerated their eager, childish inquisition and good-naturedly gave brief answers in reply. The camp dogs sniffed at Thor, but did not threaten him as they ascertained he was young and presented no threat. By the time the canoe was unloaded and secured, a heavy set man, sporting a thick growth of red hair and a beard to match, came striding down the path towards him.

Ian McPherson introduced himself as the Hudson's Bay Factor and welcomed Olaf to Hall's Landing. Olaf told him who he was and where he was located. The Factor said that he knew of him through the moccasin telegraph and had hoped they would soon meet. The Indian children were easily recruited to help pack the gear up to the trading post; hence they were rewarded with candy. Ian took Olaf to the back of the building to a small cosy bedroom where he was to be quartered while visiting. He was invited to have his meals at the Factor's home. As soon as he had settled himself, Ian told him to come over to the house and meet his wife.

The guestroom was comfortably appointed. A rustic pine, log bed, covered with a multi coloured quilt, abutted the far wall opposite the door and along side lay a braided rug to ward off the coldness of the wooden floor. The spacious window was draped with bright blue cotton curtains that pulled together for privacy. On the dressing table, a large, elaborate, kerosene lamp stood majestically on a crocheted doily. A huge porcelain wash basin and pitcher were placed on a table constructed of pine slabs. A large, shiny-black, pot-bellied stove, ready for lighting, held centre stage. The accommodation was as fine as any that could be had down south. He tidied up and presented himself at the main house.

Ian McPherson greeted Olaf and immediately escorted him into the sitting room where a warm fire was cheerfully blazing in the huge, stone fireplace. Two women arose from the sofa to meet the honoured guest. Ian first introduced Olaf to the older lady, Emma, his wife. She was a comely Indian woman, neatly dressed, with glistening black hair pulled back and tied in a bun. She had a friendly smile on her copper hued face and a happy twinkle in her dark eyes. It was apparent that the fastidiousness about her person was manifested in the manner in which she maintained their comfortable home. The younger woman was introduced as Miss Mary Hunter, the Post's schoolteacher. Mary was a tall, pretty woman with shiny, black hair that hung straight down across her shoulders like a silken curtain. Her attire was a plain white, open necked blouse tucked into a belted, black, floor length skirt. Her hazel eyes twinkled and her full lips parted to form a warm and generous smile.

Olaf was speechless and mesmerized by her beauty.

His heart raced and he could feel a hot flush come over him as she placed her warm, soft hand into his. The soft, musical lilt of her voice was like the quiet strum of an angel's harp. He was brought back to earth when Ian loudly announced that drinks were in the offing before supper. The men enjoyed several, generous nips of good, imported scotch and the ladies sipped lemonade. At this time, all were feeling very relaxed and much exchange of information about one another occurred. Thor, being allowed in, gradually worked his way to Mary and lay down by her feet, a sign that he had accepted her and she in turn stroked his ears; a mutual bond was established. After supper the men removed themselves to the sitting room to talk business while the women worked in the kitchen. Tea and biscuits were served to round off the evening. Olaf, for politeness sake, took his leave about nine o'clock. He offered to walk Mary to her home, but was disappointed to learn that she boarded with the McPhersons.

At seven o'clock, Olaf walked over to the main house to have breakfast with Mary and the McPhersons. The meal consisted of porridge, fried sowbelly and eggs from Emma's chicken house, toast with Saskatoon Berry jam and coffee. Ian said that he was going to be busy at the store for a while and suggested that Olaf walk Mary to the school. It was a short walk to the one room, log school building. Inside, there were five rows of tables with benches where the pupils sat to do their lessons. At the front of the room an old, oak desk sat to one side of the slate chalkboard. A number of windows on each side of the room let in the daylight to illuminate the blackboard and room. Kerosene lamps were hung about the room for the times when the dull winter days prevailed. A converted forty-five gallon steel barrel, centrally located in the room, was the heating system which could accommodate logs up to two feet in length. This schoolroom was not unlike the one he attended in Norway.

During his short time with Mary he learned that she was born and raised on a farm outside of Winnipeg. She started her education in a one-room school and completed her higher schooling at a girls' school in the city. She obtained a good grade standing which allowed her to teach.Hall's Landing was her first job and she has been here for two years. Olaf gave a brief outline about himself and how he chose to come to this part of the world. Many of Mary's students were beginning to arrive, so he left.

He spent the rest of the morning with Ian, arranging for the trading of his furs and selecting items to purchase. Olaf asked Ian about Bert Bates. He told him about his first encounter with the man and what he felt. Ian claimed that Bates was a renegade not to be trusted. He is suspected of raiding trap lines, stealing equipment and damaging line camps, but nothing could be proved. Also, it is rumoured that he was suspected of murdering a man down south during an argument over some property. Whenever he comes to the Post, he acts like a first class boor and is a considerable nuisance. He fancies Mary and has intimated that he would like to have her for his wife.

In regard to Pierre Duboise, Ian explained that he heard about him after he took over the Post. Pierre was, he understood, a loner and never came to the Landing very often. No, he was not a trapper, but a prospector. It was his dream to find the mother lode of gold. Sadly, he died a lonely man after two years of isolation in his cabin. It was during a vicious winter when he passed on. The harsh temperatures, minus thirty degrees, persisted for several weeks and the fall of snow was the heaviest in a decade. The frequent blizzards made travel hazardous. The wild creatures did not move about and many died due to starvation and exposure. That summer two Indians found his body. It appears that he starved to death, as there was no food in the cabin. Pieces of moose hide were sitting in an old pot. It appeared that he was boiling these to eat. Several small pieces, that were gnawed upon, rested by his emaciated body on a skin blanket. The Indians buried his remains in the woods behind the cabin. The Royal Mounted Police sergeant came in from the south and conducted an investigation at the scene. His report stated that death was due to starvation and that foul play was not suspected.

Olaf was up and about very early to ready and

load his gear. After a substantial breakfast, he thanked his hosts, said his goodbyes and stated that he would return sometime after freeze-up. He shook Mary's hand and looked into her pleasant eyes and she into his; an unspoken message secretly passed between them.

From all appearances initially, it looked as if it was going to be a reasonable day for travel. There were no indications that a change in the weather was to occur. Olaf had to paddle hard and steadily against the wind coming in from the northwest. Thor curled up into a furry ball at the bottom of the canoe to avoid the cold winds. Ahead of them, the sky had become leaden and menacing. The wind whipped up large, choppy waves and tossed freezing spray into his face, causing him to often turn his head away. He wished that he had put on his waterproof slicker at the outset, but in no way could he stop paddling to do this now as he would be in the control of the turbulence caused by the wind and choppy waves. The canoe began to lurch and bounce like a crazed bronco. It took all his muscle power to keep the craft moving forward. Travel close to shore was not a choice as the waves were severely pounding the shore. Icy, drops of rain stung his face and hands.

Up to this juncture, the exertion of paddling kept his body reasonably warm, but now the exposed parts were beginning to suffer from the cold. Olaf decided that he had no alternative but to try and get onto the shore. The wind blew fiercely and the rain turned into fat, sloppy snowflakes which stuck to his face, hands and the canoe. This presented a problem because the canoe was well loaded and the added weight caused it to settle deeper into the water. The situation was highly dangerous. Occasionally the wind dropped momentarily, allowing some vision of what lay ahead. It was during one of these moments that he caught a fleeting glimpse of a stretch of sandy white beach. He paddled frantically and desperately and angled the canoe towards it, cautiously feeling his way through the waves so as not to capsize.

When he came close to the beach, he turned directly towards it and rode the waves in, but not without shipping in some water over the stern. Olaf jumped into the knee-deep, icy water and with all his might hauled the canoe out of the reach of the incoming waves that hurtled mercilessly towards the land. Freezing sleet was pummelling his face and hands like shards of glass. The deadly cold penetrated through his clothing and seeped into his body, but he knew he could not stop until he unloaded the craft and made a shelter. It suddenly struck him that there was a familiarity about this beach. Then it dawned upon him that Pierre's cabin was back in the trees. He quickly grabbed some of the gear and scrambled to the derelict abode. Two more trips had everything under control. The canoe was overturned and tied to a tree. The cabin was an oasis in the desert.

Olaf poked around in his packs and retrieved several large candles which provided sufficient light for him to make his shelter as suitable as he could under the difficult conditions. The fireplace was still operational and, soon, he had a roaring fire going, using the old, dried logs in the wood box. He needed something hot to drink to go with the sandwiches that Emma had prepared so he donned his water-proof jacket and went out and filled the coffee pot with wet snow.

He and Thor huddled up to the fire to absorb what heat they could while they ate their lunch-come supper. Olaf had his wet outer clothing, socks and boots, draped over the firebox, chair and table, all strategically placed close to the fire. He was kept busy, until bedtime, turning the apparel to maximize the benefit of the heat. He threw several huge logs onto the fire like a sacrificial appeasement to some unknown god. The bunk bench was sturdy enough to sleep on, so the sleeping bag was unrolled without ceremony and he crawled into it, weary to the bone. Because he was so exhausted, the hard boards did not pose a problem. The last thing Olaf heard, before drifting off, was the wind howling about the cabin like a demon possessed and the icy sleet pounding the roof vengefully as if it were an attacking force trying to break its way into the cabin.

During the night the storm abated. In the morning Olaf looked out onto a landscape that looked as if Mother

Nature had gone out of her way to smother it with an icing-sugar topping. The ground was thickly layered with frozen sleet, several trees were bowed due to the weight of the ice on their branches, the lake was a mass of slush for several yards from the shore and the canoe was completely buried. The azure sky was cloudless and supported a blazing sun. Thor gingerly stepped his way around the cabin because the frozen slush was prickly on his tender pads. Olaf surmised, that after a couple of hours, the sun's warming rays will make travel possible. He savagely devoured the last of Emma's sandwiches. The canoe was easily extricated from its icy burial mound and, except for a small gash in the canvas, it suffered no other damage. He used a paddle to push a path through the heavy slush between the shore and open water.

The rest of the journey was more pleasant than yesterday's and, before he realized it, he was in his home territory. Thor began to bark excitedly as they approached the shore because some one came from the cabin and gingerly made his way to the landing. Olaf pushed the canoe through large pieces of frozen slush that looked like micro ice-burgs. As the craft slid up onto the beach, Jim Barnes was there to give him a hand. With utter surprise in his voice, Olaf asked how he got here, as there was no plane in sight. Jim explained that he was on his way back to Winnepegosis when he got caught in the storm, and, before he coulds get above it, the ice had built up on his wings and fuselage, forcing him to land. Because of the poor visibility and buffeting winds, the closest he could get to the cabin was about a half mile up the lake. Jim stated that being forced down was a blessing, because, as he was in the approach to land, the gauge indicated a drop in the oil pressure. To get above the storm, in this case, would have been disastrous. He beached the plane and secured it to a stout tree. The hardest part of the ordeal was making his way to the cabin through the blinding snow. Olaf expressed relief that Jim was safe.

The canoe was unloaded and the gear placed inside the cabin. The warmth of the cabin felt so good to Olaf. The first priority was to change into drier clothes and have a mug of hot coffee. Jim heard all about his visit to Hall's Landing and the dangers he faced between the Landing and Plerre's cabin. Jim, in turn, related how he was on his way home after making a delivery to a mining camp further north when the sudden onslaught of the storm caught him by surprise, leaving him at its mercy. He was fortunate that he was able to radio his base and put them in the picture, so they wouldn't think that he was lost or a statistic. It was agreed that tomorrow they would paddle out to where the plane was beached and asses its condition.

By mid-morning the shore ice was mostly gone and the snow was rapidly disappearing. In no time they had reached the plane. The aircraft appeared to be unharmed and most of the ice had slid off, leaving a small amount to be removed. Jim looked under the cowling to examine the condition of the motor. The only evident problem was the nut, that connected the oil line to the motor, had come loose, thus, allowing the oil to spurt out. Fortunately, a lot of oil was not lost because the motor's speed had been reduced in readiness for the landing. Jim easily tightened the nut and topped up the oil reservoir from his emergency supply. They carefully jostled the plane into the water where it could float freely and Jim taxied the craft to Olaf's beach while he followed in the canoe.

Jim judged that only four hours of daylight were left so he decided that he had better be on his way. He promised to stop by after freeze-up in early December. Olaf asked him to bring in a doll, colouring books, crayons and a big box of chocolates. He wanted these for the Christmas at Watsons. Olaf waved to Jim as the aircraft taxied across the lake and smoothly lifted off.

CHAPTER SEVEN
ATTACKED

One tedious but necessary chore that needed to be done, before trapping started, was to remove all traces of human contamination from the new steel traps. The traps were placed into a bath of boiling water and caustic potash to remove any residues of oil and human odours. Next, they were simmered in water containing logwood crystals until they turned black. He wore heavy leather gloves while handling them so no human smells remained which would probably cause an animal to shy away. Thus, gloves also needed to be worn when baiting the traps.

To lure the animal to its fateful end, the bait must be made palatable. Animals are attracted to fetid meat. Chunks of animal offal and flesh are stored in containers with lids that have tiny perforations to allow gases to escape and placed in a warm area for several days. Beaver castors are highly efficient baits. The scent glands, located at either side of the anal opening, are removed, dried, ground into a powder and mixed with glycerine, a colourless, sweet liquid. Also, freshly killed animal flesh is used to attract larger animals such as fox, wolf, cougar, bobcat and bear.

Olaf was away four days outfitting the line camps with traps and dried food. At each shack he stockpiled kindling and firewood and prepared a great number of ground stakes to which the traps were to be attached. Autumn was in full splendour; the landscape was ablaze with bright reds, yellows and rusts. He was in awe of nature's transition from summer to fall.

In the midst of readying his morning's catch of fish for the drying frame, three men had beached their birch-bark canoe at Olaf's landing. The Indians climbed from the craft, stretched their cramped muscles and then stood stoically, waiting to be greeted and welcomed. Olaf strolled down to the beach and invited the group to tea and bannock. The visitors were Anokee, Cree Chief of Fox Lake Reserve, Moses and Aaron, tribal members. The party were returning to the reserve from a trading mission at the post. Anokee mentioned that Ian, the Post Factor, suggested they stop by and become acquainted. The Chief was soft spoken and presented himself as a proud and resolute man. Over cups of tea, smoked fish and bannock a comradeship was established. The chief said that when old Angus lived here, he and the Fox Band had an understanding that they would not encroach upon his trapping, but would hunt in the area as there was sufficient game to satisfy the needs for all. Olaf replied that this was a suitable arrangement for him and he extended an open invitation for Anokee's people to stop by any time they were in the vicinity. The old chief's wrinkled, brown face broke into a wide smile and displayed worn stubs of discoloured teeth. In the Cree tongue, he passed on Olaf's words to Moses and Aaron who immediately chortled and bobbed their heads up and down vigorously in appreciation. A nod of Anokee's head signalled the two natives to rise. At this, they quickly arose and shook Olaf's hand; their leathery faces grinning from ear to ear.

During the socializing, Thor kept his distance and intently watched the visitors. When the two natives stood to shake his master's hand, he jumped in close and snarled menacingly at them. Anokee, with a practised eye, appraised Thor and stated that he would be an excellent sled dog and advised that he was at the age when training should start. A pulling harness could easily be made from strips of hide and the dog could be hooked up to pull logs suitable to his strength and then increase the load as the training progressed. He quietly suggested that in exchange for some flour and tobacco, he would have a harness and a sled made for Thor. Olaf accepted because he inwardly agreed that a sled dog would be most beneficial for his work. The chief would not accept payment at the moment, only after the outfit had been delivered. At this juncture the natives rose to take their leave, but not before Olaf presented them with gifts of dried fish, biscuits and tea which they graciously accepted. Olaf watched his new friends glide away and disappear like three ghostly spirits into the distance.

By mid November, the temperatures plummeted well below zero. Small ponds and streams froze solid and extending from the shore to the middle of the lake was a layer of rubber ice that moved up and down when cautiously walked upon, but not rigid enough to crack. Several inches of snow blanketed the land. Olaf declared to himself that winter was here to stay so he must store the canoe. Behind the cabin he built a platform, five feet off the ground, on which the overturned canoe was placed to prevent it from being buried under a mound of heavy snow. He chopped a water hole which would have to be kept open on a daily basis when in residence. Wood was hauled from his stockpile in the woods, split and piled close to the door. The meat stock was getting low so a hunt was on the agenda. That night the stormy winds gusted against the cabin walls and heavy clouds of snow swirled around like miniature tornadoes.

Grey light of the winter dawn filtered its way into the cabin through the tiny frosted windowpanes. The freezing temperature in the cabin penetrated Olaf's sleeping bag and chilled him through to the bone, causing him to awaken earlier than usual. Clouds of exhaled breath hung in the air. Thor was curled up into a tight ball with his face blanketed by his bushy tail. Olaf leapt from his bed and scurried across the frigid floor to the stove and opened the damper wide. His entire body shivered and teeth chattered uncontrollably. He stuffed the firebox with dry logs, which were quickly ignited by the smouldering, night log. He dove under the covers to await the heat to dispel the frigid, night air.

The sun, struggled to shine through a heavy sky. It was directly overhead when Olaf and Thor set out to hunt. His legs worked like pistons as he snow-shoed his way across the frozen land into the unfamiliar area up the Grass River. There were tracks of ungulates leading off into the woods where the animals were probably going to yard-up in the sheltered regions of the forest and the snow was less deep. Thor picked up a fresh spoor and let out a few excited yips. Olaf saw that it belonged to a deer and he cautioned the dog to heel so it wouldn't give chase. They proceeded along the trail slowly, ever so watchful for the animal. The sound of a dry twig snapping alerted the hunters as to where the prey was hiding. Out of the corner of his right eye, Olaf caught sight of a deer standing motionless as a statue, but poorly concealed in a growth of bare willows along the edge of an old riverbed. A well-placed shot in the region of the heart collapsed the buck as if it were a limp Raggedy Anne Doll. He gutted the deer and was in the process of tying a rope around its antlers to drag it home, when Thor began to growl and hop about as if he was standing on a hot stove.

Olaf straightened up and glanced in the direction Thor was facing. His jaw dropped and his eyes opened wide as he stared in utter astonishment. He stood rooted to the spot and watched as a huge black bear lumber with a determined gait towards him and his kill. Close behind, two ungainly cubs were striving to keep up. The mother, no doubt, had sniffed out the kill from a distance and was counting on a hearty feast before she and her babies entered hibernation. Thor foolishly gave chase to the cubs who ran behind Olaf, placing him between them and the sow, and in the heat of his excitement continued to chase them into the woods. The mother, instinctively protective, bolted with fierce energy at Olaf and knocked him to the ground with such a force that he lay stunned, face down.

She raked his back with razor sharp claws and ripped his heavy parka through to the skin. With drooling jaws agape, she was about to clamp down on his skull when the loud and frightened bawling of the distressed cubs came to her ears. Immediately, she turned away from Olaf and bounded into the woods in the direction of the cubs' crying. They were clinging to the boughs of a tree they had climbed to escape Thor's harassment. Enraged, she savagely rushed at the dog which fled from the scene as if he had been launched from a catapult. After a short chase, she returned to the tree and coaxed her off-springs to descend and, in what appeared to be utter frustration, headed off into the forest with the cubs scurrying close behind.

Thor returned to Olaf, who was beginning to rouse slowly, and nervously whined while licking at his face and hands. Olaf eased his aching body into the sitting position and glanced about in a daze. He did not know where he was or what had actually happened, but was aware that his body ached all over. He gently forced himself to his feet and stumbled about dazed, as if inebriated. Gradually, he realized what had happened and marvelled at the fact he was not more severely injured or even dead. The fact that the deer kill was undisturbed indicated that the bears had departed in a hurry. Could it have been Thor who had put them on the run; he'll never know. Slowly, and with great pain, he managed to drag the deer to the cabin and hoist it onto a limb high off the ground.

In the yellow glow from two kerosene lamps, he examined his body. The bruises on his chest, shoulders, arms and thighs looked quite angry and were very sensitive to the slightest touch. His back was hot and stinging. In the cracked mirror, by twisting his head, he was able get a view of his back. Several long, red welts stretched down from his shoulders to his waist; luckily the wounds were not open or bleeding, so no festering would likely occur. Apparently, his heavy cotton jacket and thick, wool shirt received the brunt of the bear's swipe. He mumbled that he will need to take things easy for a week to allow his body time to heal.

CHAPTER EIGHT
CARCAJOU

A heavy snow had fallen during the week Olaf was recuperating. From strips of deer hide, he made a crude harness to fit Thor. He harnessed him and then tied a small log to the trailing ends. Thor was ordered to sit while he walked some ways ahead and then called to him. When Thor ran, the weight of the log brought him to a sudden halt. He looked around in bewilderment, but did not associate the log to his dilemma. Olaf urged him to come forward and, this time, Thor pulled the log all the way to his master and was praised highly. The training exercises were made into a game between master and pet. Heavier logs were introduced gradually and Thor revelled in the ear rubs and hugs he got for his efforts. This went on for several days, two hours at a time. Eventually, Thor was hitched to a heavier log and they set out for a long hike along the shore and out upon the frozen lake. Olaf noticed that Thor was developing a deep chest and strong limbs. He was emerging from the puppy stage into a strong adult.

True to his word, Anokee had the dog sled and harness delivered. One afternoon, Moses and Aaron appeared with a team of four powerful canines pulling a large cargo sled. They were on their way to the trading post for supplies, so this was a convenient time to drop them off. It was agreed that they would pick up the flour, tea and tobacco on their way back. Olaf told them that if they did not return by the time he left for his trap line, the goods would be just inside the door and they could they could fire up the stove and brew up some tea and help themselves to hard tack and jam. This gesture was warmly accepted and thus the bond of friendship and trust was strengthened. They then sped away down the embankment and out onto the lake. Like two shadowy ghosts, they disappeared from sight into the wisps of spiralling snow that were stirred up as they rounded the spit jutting into the lake.

There was a tinge of slate grey to the overcast sky when Olaf and Thor left for the line camps. The sled was loaded with food, tools, gun and a miscellany of other items needed for the trapping expedition. Olaf broke the trail with his snowshoes thus allowing Thor to pull his load with less difficulty. The deep snow had obscured the trail, so he relied on the blazes he made in the fall. They reached the camp in three hours. The threat of snow was imminent, so he scurried around to get the camp organized before the storm descended. Within the hours of daylight left, Olaf set four beaver traps under the ice of the pond and five smaller traps around the shore for marten and weasel. The pair were comfortably settled in their digs when heavy, fat flakes, which capered about crazily ahead of the gusting, polar winds, started to fall. The wind attacked the tiny, cosy shelter as if it were a crazed demon resentful of it being there. During the night the blizzard raged throughout the land, piling up huge snowdrifts against any object that dared to obstruct its path. In the first light of dawn, Olaf shoved open the door, pushed the drift aside, and stepped out into knee deep snow. The land was unrecognisable. The storm had covered it with a blanket of pure whiteness and the still, icy air had an atmosphere of heavy silence. He felt certain that the land traps would have been undisturbed during the night because of the storm, but the under water traps may have caught something. After a breakfast of cold bannock and moose jerky, he visited the beaver pond to check the traps. Their locations were easy to find because the long, tree limbs he stuck into the snow by the traps were poking out above the drifts. Only one trap was successful; it caught him a small, young male beaver. Out of curiosity, he checked the land traps and, to his delight, three weasels were caught. Their fur was as white as the newly fallen snow. Before he stopped for the day, Olaf had set ten large and twelve small traps within a mile radius of the camp. He and Thor enjoyed the warmth of the fire inside the shack while their meal was simmering in the pot. When the sun dipped below the treetops, it was time to settle in for the night. The glowing embers in the fire pit gave off a comforting warmth and a cheery glow. A plentiful supply of dry logs was at hand to feed the fire during the night.

They headed out for camp Number Two when there was enough morning light to allow them to travel. The trail had to be broken for Thor and his load. The sun was a finger width above the treetops when they arrived. After a hearty breakfast, most of the day was spent in setting traps. Close to where he had set a large trap, he noticed, in the shallow snow beside a pine tree, several piles of bear scat. Bears are in the habit of cleansing their bowels before hibernating. This practice is carried out in an area close to their winter lair. Olaf scouted the area and soon found the bear's den situated under a heavy windfall of dead trees against the side of a hill and covered over by a dome of snow. Tiny puffs of vapour were emanating from a small air hole at the top of the mound, pinpointing the bear's winter sanctuary. He did not disturb the occupant at this time, but made a mental note as to where the den was located. During the night the temperature had dropped considerably and Olaf wakened on the hour throughout the night to feed the fire. He struck camp well before daylight and headed out for Dead Bear Camp. A full moon dominated the cloudless sky and lit the forest trail like a bright lantern. Ice crystals hung in the frigid air and his breath froze on the fur of his hood and on his collar. It was difficult to breathe properly under such conditions, so he was forced to stop often to prevent his lungs becoming frost burned. It was a strenuous three hours, but eventually the camp came into view and both travellers lunged forward over the last hundred yards and collapsed in a heap at the door.

When they got their second wind, Olaf fired up the stove to heat the shack and cooked a much-needed breakfast. By the time they were ready to go out and set the traps, the sun had risen well above the trees. Soon its meagre, winter warmth would make getting around a little more tolerable. Rabbit trails were everywhere so he set several snares. At the end of the day, Olaf retrieved four plump rabbits, which were roasted over the hot coals and thoroughly enjoyed. While resting by the fire, he reflected on the strange tracks he saw on his rounds earlier. They were deep and wide as if a small plough had passed through. This puzzled him because he did not know what sort of animal made them. On the homeward journey, the sled carried eleven frozen carcasses of mink, marten and muskrat and three prime fox skins. Because the foxes were caught in leg traps, they were still alive, so Olaf put them out of their misery with a sharp blow to the head and skinned them right there on the trail while their bodies were still warm and easy to work.

When they were within two miles of home, Olaf noticed smoke spiralling into the clear skies above the treetops where his cabin was located. He wondered who might be visiting. When he came around the last bend on the approach to the house, he saw six sled dogs tethered amongst the trees and a sled on its side along the front wall. The dogs all raised their voices in a chorus of howls as Thor and Olaf neared the cabin. The door flung open and he saw the silhouette of a huge person standing in the dimly lit entrance. Moses erupted from the doorway to greet Olaf and explained that he and his brother had to stop over for several days because Aaron had an accident and hurt his back. It happened as they were cautiously descending a steep, icy slope. The sled went out of control and Aaron, the driver, plummeted to the bottom where his back slammed against a tree. The pain made movement unbearable. They got as far as the cabin and stopped over so Aaron could rest. Inside, Olaf found Aaron propped up on the bunk bed with his back against the wall. He said that there was still some pain, but was feeling somewhat better. Olaf examined his back and diagnosed, to the best of his ability, that no bones were broken, but believed that his back muscles were badly strained. He bound Aaron's back and chest firmly with some old cloth which allowed him the freedom of movement with reasonable comfort. After a sumptuous meal, the three men relaxed in idle talk and puffed on their pipes. Olaf mentioned, that on his run to Dead Bear Camp, he came across the track of an animal that was a mystery to him and when he described it, they both, simultaneously, burst out that it was the track of Carcajou, the highly dreaded wolverine. Moses went on to say that the wolverine was the largest member of the weasel family, about the size of a bear cub. It feeds on small mammals1, carrion, birds, fish, fruit, roots and attacks animals caught in traps. It sprays whatever it does not consume with a thick, putrid, musk substance similar to that of skunks, thus it is referred to as the skunk-bear. They are a costly nuisance to a trapper because they have been known to travel a trap-line and deliberately destroy and foul the trapped animals. Should they ever find a way to enter a cabin they will wilfully trash the cabin contents and spray their offensive secretion all about. Though highly cursed by trappers, they were sought after for their fur. It is highly desired for the trim on parka hoods, as frost and ice crystals do not adhere to it. One swipe with the hand completely dislodges the frost. A trapper would be fortunate in more ways than one if he could kill or trap the elusive wolverine. A sense of uneasy concern came over Olaf when he heard about the terrible weasel.

Aaron spoke about Bert Bates, the crazy trapper as the Indians called him. When they were at the trading post, Bert went on a drinking binge and was a first class, obnoxious nuisance to all at the post. He verbally abused and threatened them because they were Indians. He vowed he would kill all Indians that crossed his path and hang their bodies from a tree as a lesson to all that follow. Bart bragged that the teacher, Mary Hunter, was his woman and one day she would become his wife. The residents of the settlement became very alarmed and frightened by his behaviour. In a drunken rage, he shot a dog that had wandered across his path. Sergeant Lee Williams of the RCMP and two strong male members of the community forcibly restrained him and locked him up in the police barrack's cell. He has been banned from visiting the trading post except to purchase supplies or trade his furs. He would not be allowed to linger within the settlement proper once his transactions were complete. Bates did not take kindly to this decree and swore to avenge this treatment. Olaf feared for Mary's safety.

The Indians left Olaf's place long before sunup. They urged him to visit their reserve this winter. They told him that the winter trail would be wide and well packed for travelling. He could easily find it by going north along the west shore, through the narrows into Herblet lake, past the opening of the long bay that goes to Watson's camp and continue north until he sees a lone spruce tree standing at the mouth of a wide creek. There he will find the trail heading north westerly to their home. On the east side of the lake, they cautioned, is a trail that follows Cutter's Creek into Bert's camp, it would be best for him to stay off that trail.

Olaf spent two, busy days tending to the skins and camp chores. The small animals had to be thawed, skinned, scraped clean and stretched. From his meat stores he cut a large chunk of deer rump and put it into the oven to roast while he went about his work. He also wrote a letter to his family; ready to be sent out with Jim the next time he comes. Even though he was constantly busy, he could not remove from his thoughts the peculiar and threatening behaviour of Bert Bates who, he firmly believed, was deranged and one could not let down his guard with him. He came to the realization that he loved Mary and wanted her to become his wife. The more he thought about it, the more apprehensive he became over her well being.

December moved on and Olaf was anxious to get the trap line organized and then make a visit to the trading post before his Christmas visit with the Watsons. He made a three-day trip around his trapping route to collect the animals that had been caught. In all, he was pleased with the fur harvest, six mink, four muskrats, one ermine, two foxes and a bobcat. The foxes and bobcat had to be put out of their misery. The traps were not reset because he would be away for two to three weeks.

When they reached Camp One on their homeward journey, Olaf felt as if his heart had popped up into his throat because he could see the definite signs of Carcajou's visit. The snow was trampled all around the shack and he saw that the beast had forced open the flimsy door. The supply of candles had been chewed beyond use and the sack that held the emergency supply of moose jerky was lying on the floor, torn to shreds. It looked as if a cyclone had passed through. The dirt floor, fire circle, walls and spruce-bough bedding were completely ravaged in a most maniacal way and the unmistakable, strong, foul stench of the wolverine's spray hung heavily in the air. He exited the shack on the double because his eyes smarted terribly and he gagged and choked. How right the Indians were when they called that obnoxious weasel the "Skunk Bear". The shelter could not be used again so a new one will have to be built in a location some distance away. The cunning wolverine had now become the dreaded enemy who must be destroyed. The sun had plummeted out of view and the winter's dusk settled over the land like a shroud long before they reached the cabin.

A sub-arctic system moved in overnight and temperatures throughout the land hovered well below sub-zero for several days. Each morning, the land was shrouded in an ice-crystal, laced fog until the sun reached its mid-point. During these days, while they were confined to the cabin, Olaf prepared the hides, repaired equipment, baked bread, cooked meat dishes and cleaned the cabin. By the day's end he looked forward to some well earned relaxation; smoking his pipe, reading and listening to the radio.

They were well on their way along the trail to Hall's Landing before the sun had hinted at making an appearance over the trees. He went ahead of Thor and broke trail. At times they would swing out onto the lake and cut across a bay to save time and distance. It was during one of these moments that they spotted a wolf pack running along the far shore. The pack was not interested in them because they were in hot pursuit of a moose, which was stretching out its long limbs to escape the vicious, killing horde. Olaf watched as the wolves shortened the distance between them and their quarry. The moose lost all chances to escape, because the deep snowdrifts bogged him down to a standstill. In an instant the pack descended upon him en masse. The animal met his demise beneath a heavy blanket of snarling beasts, who literally tore at his body with razor-sharp fangs. Olaf understood that this was the way of nature and could not condemn the action, after all, he too is a hunter of the moose for sustenance. Young Thor, quivering with fear, watched the drama of life and death as he snuggled against his master's legs. When the command to mush was given, Thor bolted, pulling mightily on his load, as if the devil was after him. The sun was directly over-head, barely visible through the translucent clouds, when they halted for a mug-up. The blackened tea pail was packed tightly with snow and then hung over a blazing fire. When the snow-water came to a boil, a generous handful of tea leaves was chucked in and the brew was set to the side of the fire to steep and keep hot. The warmth of the fire and a full stomach lulled Olaf into a catnap. Fully refreshed, they resumed their journey with renewed vigour. As the long afternoon wore on, the effects of the dropping temperature were more acutely felt, thus he picked up the pace as he wanted to reach Pierre's cabin before nightfall. They stayed on the lake, close to the shoreline, where the wind had packed the snow hard, and made better time. The only drawback to this was that a stiff breeze was constantly blowing down the length of the lake and sending up clouds of sharp, snow crystals, which, at times, obliterated the way ahead. Eventually, after what seemed an eternity, the derelict shack was spotted amongst the trees at the end of the narrow bay. It was dark by the time they were settled, as best could be, within the less than perfect surroundings. As the night progressed, the temperature dropped dramatically, so he had to sit near the fire all night in order to keep adding logs, as needed. Wrapped in a blanket, he propped himself against the wall and cat napped in between stoking the fire. He groggily awakened as the dim rays of the early morning light gently penetrated the gloomy interior. After a hurried, cold breakfast, camp was struck.

It was midday when he saw fluffy curls of smoke lazily rising from the black metal chimneys at Hall's Landing. The Post dogs announced his arrival long before he reached the landing. Ian McPherson beamed from ear to ear when he saw Olaf. He shook his hand warmly and stated how glad he was to see him. Four native men were huddled around the huge, cast-iron, pot bellied stove quietly chatting as if they were having a clandestine meeting. Two squaws were rummaging through the gaudy bolts of material at the far end, appearing ever so serious about which colours to select. The warmth that permeated through the store gradually drove the chill from Olaf's body. His nostrils sucked in the pleasant odours of groceries, hardware, tanned leather, damp parkas and pipe smoke. He greeted the natives with a nod of his head and they stoically nodded back and grunted an equivalent Cree hello. Ian helped to put the gear into the guestroom at the back of the store and then invited him to tea in his office. The two men exchanged their respective pieces of news. Ian brought up the incidence with Bert Bates and added that he was spotted in a camp several miles north of the village and this has the community somewhat concerned. The two friends were so engrossed in conversation they did not realize it was time to close shop. Ian invited him to supper. Olaf said he would be over as soon as he washed and changed. His heart was pounding in anticipation of seeing Mary. Before leaving his room, he banked up the fire in the stove and set the damper so the fire would burn slowly and still put out some heat.

Mary greeted him at the door and they both smiled warmly at each other. Olaf held her warm, tender hands and the touch sent a tingle up his spine and made him shiver with delight. As he momentarily held her hand, he gazed into her soft, hazel eyes. Her beautiful, round face, framed by tresses of shiny, black, silken hair, blushed slightly and when she peered into his dark eyes, her ruby, red lips formed into a coquettish smile. As they entered the living room, Ian and Emma could not help but notice the glow of happiness that radiated from them. The evening of dining and visiting passed all too quickly. Ian and Emma excused themselves on the pretence of being tired and ready for bed and said goodnight to the young couple. The love-struck ones sat on the couch close to each other and quietly talked about their dreams, likes, dislikes, fears, desires and, most important, they openly declared their feelings, which were deeper than just friendly. The dim light from the glowing fire created an ideal romantic atmosphere. The clock chimed the midnight hour and Olaf reluctantly made ready to depart. At the door, he held Mary in a tender embrace and kissed her soft, accepting lips. On the way to his quarters, he felt as buoyant as a feather in the wind. He and Thor raced jubilantly across the snow, leaping into the air like two carefree elves.

Olaf walked Mary to school and spent a half-hour with her before the students arrived. They embraced and kissed and he said he would come for her at the end of the school day. The rest of the morning was spent with Ian at the store. After conducting his business and lunch, he strolled through the sparse village and acquainted himself with its layout. There was an assortment of old, grey, board buildings; some encircled with tired looking picket fences and others standing aloof from the road.

Only a few had windows adorned with curtains and painted outer walls that gave them a faint semblance to city style houses. The other buildings were the school, RCMP (Royal Canadian Mounted Police Detachment), Catholic Church, Factor's House and the Trading Post. Olaf called at the Police Detachment and introduced himself to Sergeant Lee Williams. He learned that Lee's jurisdiction covered a large area around and beyond Herb Lake. The recent incident with Bert Bates was discussed and Williams confirmed Olaf's feelings and opinions. He stated that Bert was a renegade trapper who, it is certain, will seriously overstep the boundary's of the law. When that time comes, he will be very difficult to apprehend and subdue because he is very violent and unpredictable. The Sergeant mentioned, that in the New Year, he would be on his winter patrol to check out some mining operations north of Herblet Lake and asked if he may stop by to visit. Olaf invited Lee to stay overnight anytime and, if he happened to be out on his trap line, to make use of the cabin and its contents.

When he saw the children leave the school, he left the detachment and went to meet Mary and escorted her home. As they walked, he asked Mary if she was in any way concerned about or afraid of Bert Bates. Mary replied that she is not and since its their last evening together, they should not bother their heads about such an imbecile. Olaf expressed his concerns and asked that she be alert at all times, as threats from a deranged person should not be taken lightly. The evening gathering with the McPhersons and Mary went by too quickly to suit him. He and Mary hugged and kissed affectionately as they said their good nights. Olaf told her that he loved her. Mary gently stroked his face with her delicate fingers and whispered that she knew and she loved him.

The sullen, grey shadows of the murky dusk were infiltrating the forest as they pulled up to Pierre's shack. His first task was to gather a supply of logs for the fire. Soon a roaring fire was ablaze and sparks flew about like miniature exploding firecrackers. After supper, Olaf stepped outside to view the night sky. The moon, shining like a brilliant floodlight, lit up the contrasting white and dark landscape making the vista before him breathtaking. The night temperature had dipped well below zero, and this meant another night of sitting up, feeding the fire and catnapping in between. He sat contentedly before the fire smoking his pipe and sipping coffee. Many thoughts permeated his mind, but the most frequent ones were those of Mary. His heart speeded up when he thought about her and he felt so fortunate that she loved him in return. The warmth of the flames dispelled the cold and the fatigue of the day's journey. Olaf and Thor slipped ever so easily out of the harshness of the real world into the comforting arms of sleep. Several times during the long night, icy fingers stealthily crept over his body forcing him to awaken and fuel the fire. He felt that the depth of coldness this night was the most extreme he has experienced to date. The walls of the cabin creaked and several tree trunks exploded with the intensity of rifle shots. At the first light of day, Thor's deep-throated growls and gruff woofs roused Olaf, an indication that something was agitating him. It took a moment to rub the sleep out of his eyes and, when they became focussed, he saw two moose staring intensely through the black hole of the window frame. The moment was opportune to bring one of them down to replenish his larder, but the thoughts of preparing the carcass in the freezing temperature and the tremendous chore of transporting it home were enough to quickly dispel the notion. He let out a tremendous yell which startled the beasts. They bound away into the woods and disappeared like phantoms in the frosty mist. Without the luxury of a meal, they struck out for home as soon as the sun lighted their way. They made good time travelling along the edge of the frozen lake, and, with only one stop for a quick mug-up, they arrived home by mid afternoon.

Olaf put the kindling and fire logs together and soon had the stove ablaze like a three-alarm fire. While the cabin was being heated, he grabbed his axe and two pails and went down to the lake for water. It took him ten minutes to chop through the ice that covered the water hole to a thickness of about six inches. He had worked up a sweat during the effort, but, as soon as he finished, the frigid breeze turned the perspiration into ice water on his body. A hasty retreat to the cabin got him in out of the cold. He quickly removed the damp clothing and snuggled up to the stove and the waves of hot air caressed his shivering body. Each piece of fresh dry clothing was held close to the fire to dispel their coldness before he donned them. The smell of the moist clothing, hanging on a makeshift line was not unlike that of wet chicken feathers. Tomorrow, he will do the laundry. After supper, he had a thorough wash from head to toe and an invigorating rub down with the towel. The full moon was shining through wispy clouds that scudded across the star lit sky when he eased his tired body under the blankets. He doused the lamp and said goodnight to Thor who was cuddled into his own body at the foot of the bed. His heavy lids dropped like heavy stage curtains, his body twitched and his whole being succumbed to a deep sleep.

The drying clothes created the ambience of a Chinese laundry. When thoroughly dry, he laid each item of clothing on the table and passed the flat of his hand over them for a mediocre pressing. Other chores for the day were to bank more snow around the outside walls, split wood, tidy up the cabin and get ready for the trap lines. Olaf baked a large pot of beans, made a batch of biscuits and fried up several round moose steaks. He portioned the beans into meal sizes and put them out to freeze and then wrapped them in a clean tea towel. On the trap line he would place a slab of beans into the pot with snow and cook over the fire. The biscuits were placed into a drawstring bag for accessibility. The moose steaks were cut into strips about one by four inches. On the trail they could be thrown in with beans or eaten cold. Through the water hole, he jigged for trout and was rewarded with two large ones. Fried trout, boiled rice and cranberry sauce sated his appetite. To make the sauce he soaked the dried berries for several hours. He then sugared the mix and let it simmer until the mixture thickened into a jam consistency.

In case he missed Jim, Olaf left him a note stating that he would be away for four days and to leave the goods on the bunk bed and asked him to mail the letter to his family. He hoped that they would not miss each other, as it would be some time before they will see each other again.

They arrived at Camp One just before noon. Olaf's hair bristled as he viewed the destruction the wolverine had meted out spitefully and wilfully on his crude dwelling. He selected a spot well away from the old hut to make a camp. He scooped away the deep snow using a snow shoe as a spade, erected a lean-to, put up a log, heat reflecting barrier on the opposite side of the fire, laid down a layer of spruce boughs for his bed and readied the camp fire with kindling and dry branches. A good supply of logs was hauled in from the bush.

The last trap was set in the dusk and finding their way back to camp was a slow process as the trails were not well defined. Olaf congratulated himself for having the foresight to prepare the camp beforehand. The bean and moose steak stew was a delight to wolf down with biscuits to sop the gravy. He would have liked some butter and jam, but they would have frozen solid in this weather. The fire was fuelled and soon the multicoloured flames were leaping and dancing frantically as sparks exploded into the darkness. Handy to his bed, he had a supply of dry logs to throw onto the fire without having to rise during the night. Cocooned in the wool blankets, he quickly slipped into the land of nod.

Olaf made an early start in the pre-dawn light under intermittent clouds that were building up to the north. The deep snow on the trail made travelling cumbersome. After three long hours of strenuous trail breaking, they reached the second camp. It looked like a gingerbread house covered in a thick layer of icing. Looking about, he was satisfied that every thing was intact. Soon a hot fire was blazing in the sheet metal stove. A belated breakfast and hot coffee set things right. Olaf spent until dusk setting traps. He anticipated a good harvest as there were numerous animal trails interweaving throughout the forest. Tomorrow they will proceed to Dead Bear Camp and spend two nights in order to check the traps. At the camp there were signs of an animal trying to force entry, but fortunately, when he refurbished it, he reinforced the structure and door with heavy timbers. He knew it could not have been a bear as they were in hibernation. Although the signs were quite old, the depth and width of the tracks and the strong, skunk odour convinced him that it was the hated weasel's calling card. Without delay, he went about the task of setting traps. The clouds coming in from the north were bunching up and it was not long before fat, white flakes flitted about; gently at first, but within a half hour they filled the sky as if the clouds had been ripped open and their contents dumped relentlessly. Olaf and Thor slogged their way back to camp through the ever-deepening snow. While they slept, the steady, silent fall of snow laid down a heavy blanket of white over the landscape which muffled all sounds.

By morning the storm had passed. Olaf used the door to push the deep snow away from the entrance. The branches of the pines were loaded with what looked like globs of vanilla ice cream. Any slight breeze would be enough to dislodge the snow and cause it to plop heavily upon unsuspecting trappers and animals. After breakfast, he set out to do the rounds of the trap line. Breaking trail was difficult, so occasional stops were required. Thor put up a valiant effort to keep, but there were occasions when he lagged behind because the sled slid off the trail. Fresh spoor was spotted along the trail. One, which deeply concerned him looked like the tracks of Carcajou. This was ominous, and his whole being switched into a high state of alertness; his muscles tensed, he listened intensely and his eyeballs darted up, down and sideways as if they were on swivels. The first three traps yielded him two marten and a muskrat; all wore prime pelts. Unfortunately, in the next two traps their victims had been torn to shreds and sprayed. Olaf's heart beat heavily like a drum. His throat tightened and anger welled within him like a rushing, incoming tide. He became very determined in his resolve to destroy this hateful creature from hell. In all he retrieved nine whole animals, one a fine, white fox. A total of five catches were destroyed and the traps made useless until they could be disinfected.

On their return to Dead Bear Camp, Thor suddenly stopped dead and stared into the bush and emitted a combination of throaty growls and whimpers. This action caused Olaf to stop and look back. He slowly scanned the area in the direction Thor was looking and, suddenly, the Skunk Devil zoomed into view. He looked like a life sized carving, standing so still, gazing directly into Olaf's eyes without trepidation. It was deep brown in colour with the telltale, light buff coloured band running from the front to the rear, midway between the back and belly. There they stood, man and beast, eyes flashing deep hatred at one another. He slowly eased the rifle to his shoulder, took aim and ever so carefully squeezed the trigger. To his utmost surprise, the bullet entered the log exactly where Carcajou had been standing. The elusive weasel vanished into the forest quicker than Olaf could blink. He cursed his bad luck and trembled, not with the cold, but with fury at himself for missing. They reached Dead Bear Camp in the cold, bleak darkness.

They arrived back home after being away for a week. Olaf was pleased with the results of his trapping. He did not reset the traps because he would not be back until after his visit to the Watsons over Christmas. Life around the camp for the next week was relaxed. He prepared his pelts, stocked the wood supply, cleaned the cabin and baked some bread. He and Thor went out for an afternoon's hunt and came back with a fat doe. His meat larder was now in a better state. Through the water hole, he hooked two fat lake trout and a large whitefish that were an added change to the diet. One afternoon when he was getting water, he heard the drone of a distant plane flying northward. He thought it might be Jim Barnes flying supplies into the miners and trappers further north. Jim, he was certain, will drop down on his way back to Winnepegosis. Olaf returned to the cabin and made preparations for his Christmas trip to the Watsons. He had just finished chopping and stacking his fire logs when his ears detected a faint, dull drone that increased in volume as the minutes passed. When he looked upwards, towards the direction of the sound, a plane suddenly burst from behind a mass of grey clouds and began its descent. Jim eased the craft gently onto the hard packed surface of the lake and, when the skis gently kissed the snow, he throttled back the engine and the plane glided to a stop. He gunned the motor and the craft swung right around and skipped its way over the small, snow hummocks towards the shore up to where Olaf and Thor were standing. The two men greeted each other warmly. No time was wasted before they started to unload the supplies and haul them up to the cabin. Jim had time to have a visit and enjoy some coffee and cranberry bannock. They had a lot of news to exchange since their last visit. Olaf recounted the episode of Bert Bates at the trading post. Jim added that anything he heard about the scoundrel was not good. He gave Jim a letter to mail and an order for supplies to be delivered when he returned sometime in mid January. As the aircraft sped across the lake to obtain lift-off speed it churned up a powerful blizzard that obscured it from sight until it left the lake and slowly rose over the horizon and became a dot in the distance.

With the supplies put away and the venison stew on the simmer at the back of the stove, Olaf turned his attention to the mail. He opened a neatly wrapped parcel from his family. It contained a letter, knitted socks, scarf, toque, mitts and a pullover sweater, all embellished with the traditional Norwegian designs. He remembered Christmases past where the brothers would receive the annual woollen wear, diligently and secretly knitted by their mother. His thoughts were of home. He missed the family, especially at this time of the year. Tears slowly drained down his cheeks and fell onto his laps like dewdrops from a blade of grass. He read about the events in their lives and that all was well, except his father, Gustav, was suffering from arthritis in the joints of his fingers and knees. He gets around with the aid of two canes. Svend, the older of the brothers, is going to be married in September to Olga, his childhood sweetheart. They will build a home on the property and help the father work the farm. Larsen, the youngest, is still attending high school and is able to help during the weekends and holidays. His mother's sight is failing, so she is wearing glasses for the first time in her life, otherwise she would not be able to carry on with her reading and needlepoint. Each member of the family personally wrote several lines and wished him well and a very Merry Christmas. The second letter was from his friend, Stefan. He wrote that all was well and the farm was prospering with the up-to-date techniques he was applying and he had hired a young lad to work full time with him. His mother was eighty-five and failing. Her blood pressure was quite high and difficult to control. Due to this condition she had a blood vessel burst in her left eye, causing a loss of vision. Stefan expressed his hope that they would meet again sometime in the future. Olaf spotted a cardboard box on the bed. His curiosity aroused, he carefully opened it to preserve the paper and twine. Inside, he found the doll, colouring book, crayons and the big box of chocolates. As well, Jim had enclosed a 1921 calendar with a wildlife animal picture for each month. On the January page, as if to taunt him, was a large black and white photo of a wolverine, with glaring, evil eyes. Further, to his great surprise, there were two bottles of over-proof Hudson's Bay Rum, Christmas compliments of Jim. Olaf slumped into his chair; grinned and exclaimed aloud that this has been a wonderful day.

As Olaf and Thor came within sight of Watson's cabin, they could hear the dogs barking up a storm, and what a wonderful sound that was after hours of steady snowshoe travel through the cold stillness and silence of the wilderness. William was at the landing, watching as they approached. From a distance the men hollered greetings to one another and the dogs yipped excitedly. Betty and Josie were at the door to welcome Olaf while Thor and his siblings raced and tumbled about like happy children on recess break. The cabin's cosy warmth enveloped him as he entered and, within, he could hear the stove humming as the blazing fire greedily consumed the logs and, in the corner by the window, he saw a tall spruce tree adorned with decorations made from paper and scraps of coloured cloth. Several gifts, wrapped in plain paper, were tidily tucked beneath its sweeping branches. A mellow glow from four kerosene lamps, strategically placed, bathed the cabin in an ethereal light. Momentarily, Olaf felt homesick, as the atmosphere brought to mind the love and happiness he enjoyed with his family during past Christmas seasons.

After a substantial snack of fresh baked bread, slices of cold, roast moose, raisin biscuits and copious cups of steaming coffee, the group sat and chatted. Olaf expounded about his trapping, Carcajou, the visits by the Indians, training Thor to pull a sled, the troublesome Bert Bates, and lastly he told them about Mary Hunter and his feelings for her. William and Betty were delighted and playfully teased him about an imminent wedding. The Watsons, in turn, told him their news. William had a successful run with his trapping and he also had a brush with a wolverine that defiled some of his catches. The beast was wary around baited traps and deftly eluded William's rifle shots. Eventually it left the area, never to be seen again. Possibly, Olaf had inherited the devil from him. Young Josie remained healthy this winter and was doing well with her home schooling. Betty and Josie retired to their beds, but Olaf and William stayed up and quietly talked and sipped on hot rum toddies. It was midnight when the two men, fully relaxed and tired, made ready for bed. The dogs were called in and they fussed about momentarily. William's dogs lay behind the stove and Thor curled up at the foot of Olaf's sleeping bag on the floor.

Christmas morning started with a bustle of activity. The dogs were scampering about like wound up plush toys eager to get outside and, as soon as they crowded through the door, they immediately started to bark at and methodically sniff around for some imaginary intruder. Mary laid out a light breakfast of toast, jam and coffee. The below freezing temperature outside was inconsequential to the happy people inside, surrounded by a cloak of warmth. The highlight of the morning was the opening of gifts. Josie squealed in happy anticipation as she carefully unwrapped her treasures. From her parents she received a blue pinafore dress, knitted scarf and mitts and a small, pine, log rocking chair that had been laboriously handcrafted during the winter evenings when she was fast asleep. Her eyes stared in disbelief at the gifts Olaf had given her. She immediately fell in love with the doll, which she quickly named Dolly, and was overjoyed with the huge, thick colouring book and crayons. Betty and William voiced their appreciation for the chocolates that were offered around. William announced that their gift could not be wrapped because it would not sit still long enough. They presented him with one of Thor's siblings to add to his team. Each dog has been trained in harness for pulling and he could take his pick. Olaf's initial look of surprise changed to one of delighted pleasure. He graciously thanked the family and said that he could not have received a nicer and more practical gift. Betty and William exchanged their gifts, a pan of brown sugar fudge for William's sweet tooth and a pine foot-stool for Betty to keep her feet off the cold floor when she sat on her favourite chair.

Betty and Josie prepared a sumptuous Christmas dinner of standing rib-roast of moose, powdered mash potatoes, canned peas and carrots, fresh baked rolls and raisin-cranberry pie. With appetites satisfied and bellies that were as taut as drums, the group left the table to relax by the stove. The adults lazily conversed while Josie played with her new possessions.

The sun, well past its zenith, glowed weakly like a lantern in a fog when all evidence of the recent feast was cleared away. William and Olaf dragged themselves away from the comfort of the cabin to do some outdoor chores before nightfall. They fed the dogs, split firewood, chopped open the water hole and hauled several pails of water. The rest of the evening was spent leisurely talking, snacking and drinking coffee laced with rum. William stated that he would be making a trip to the post in three weeks time, a trip he makes twice a year, winter and late summer. Betty and Josie stay home during the winter, but in summer they all made the journey. Olaf suggested that he come by and spend the night, then they could go on together. He had planned to go in January to see Mary and get supplies. Olaf said that he would be on the trap line for two weeks, but would be back to his cabin before the end of the third week.

Olaf selected a sturdy, energetic dog from William's team. She had the black, beige and tan markings of a husky with erect pointed ears, but slightly smaller than Thor. William still had his original sled harness he used when running only two dogs. They tandem hitched Thor and Kyla to the sled loaded with about two hundred pounds of cut logs and made a trial run through the bush and across the snow packed bay. The team performed very well. Thor pulled like a trooper in the lead position and Kyla easily fell into line as the rear dog. William provided Olaf some guidance in teaching Thor the commands a lead dog must understand. The sled's runners extended far enough back to allow the musher to stand on and ride.

At daybreak, when Olaf left his friends, a steady, icy wind was blowing fiercely down the bay and across the lake. Sullen clouds were scudding across the horizon like galleons plunging through angry waves. He feared that it might snow before he got home, so no mug-up stops were planned. Travel across the wind packed snow on the lake was smooth and rapid. The dogs ran in unison at a steady pace and 0laf was able to ride the runners for most of the way. By mid afternoon, the heavy, dark clouds, hovering low, curtained off the light from the sun, thus turning day into dusk. The wind played cat and mouse with the travellers. It would fiercely attack, tugging at them and threw up clouds of icy snow into their faces and in an instant it would stop, as if it had run away to molest elsewhere, only to return too quickly and further harass the weary travellers. The temperature had plummeted considerably in a short space of time and tiny snowflakes began to fall like tossed confetti. Gusts of arctic air piled the loose snow into hillocks on the lake's surface. The snowfall and wind increased in intensity which created near whiteout conditions and reduced his visibility. Conditions were worsening, so he headed for the trees while he could still see, otherwise, he could lose his bearings and end up travelling in the wrong direction. They struggled through the drifts along the shore and laboriously made their way into the shelter of the forest where the wind was considerably reduced in severity and the snowfall less intense. In the failing light, he managed to stumble onto the home trail. After several hours of gruelling work, they eventually broke from the dark forest and entered the clearing wherein the lonely, snow covered cabin stood, a haven in the storm. What a glorious sight, thought Olaf, as he peered at it through ice-crusted eyelids. It was not long before he had the lamps lit, the stove ablaze and the sled unpacked. He ploughed his way through the drifting snow to the water hole and chopped it open with great effort. With the two pails full to the brim, he struggled back to the cabin. During the night the wind angrily buffeted the cabin and the snow crept higher and higher against the cabin walls, as if it had wanted to obliterate it from the world.

CHAPTER NINE
ABDUCTION AND MURDER

Olaf returned from his trap line four days ahead of the rendezvous time with William. January, thus far, had been an exceedingly cold month which made his task more difficult. However, his efforts were amply rewarded. He brought home a total of twenty-three pelts but the highlight of the trip was that one of the twenty-three was Carcajou's hide. On the way home, they came across the distinctive tracks of the skunk devil leading off in the direction they were travelling. Inwardly, Olaf cursed and began to wonder if his foe had extra sensory perception about when he would be on his line. Snow shoeing ahead of the dogs, he peered intently for any hidden dangers that may be ahead. Because the snow was powdered and deep, their movements were muffled, making their progress almost soundless. The Devil Weasel had veered sharply off the trail and ploughed a deep furrow through the snow, and, in all appearances, it seemed to be in a hurry. He halted and carefully scanned the area into which the wolverine's tracks had disappeared. The only audible sound in the eerie silence was the rapid panting of the dogs and his laboured breathing. Clouds of frozen moisture floated momentarily in front of their faces. After several moments of intense silence, Olaf turned and headed down the trail with Thor and Kyla in tow. They had not gone more than twenty paces when a sudden outburst of vicious snarling, barking, and throaty growls erupted from within the woods. He tied the dogs to a tree, grabbed the rifle and proceeded cautiously along the trail made by Carcajou. The trail snaked its way through the forest and crossed a large meadow that dipped into a deep ravine before it rose abruptly to a flat, sparsely treed bench land. From the ravine, loud sounds of animals viciously fighting emanated. In order to view the situation, he crept on hands and knees through the deep snow to the rim and slowly pushed his head over and peered down. A savage wilderness drama was being played out. He saw the weasel engaged in a serious battle with two young wolves. The prize being fought over was the carcass of a fat, partly eaten, mule deer. The wolverine stood its ground against the wolves by keeping its back against a huge rock and countering their attacks with forward lunges and snapping jaws. He saw that it was a formidable adversary and he inwardly admired it for its tenacious spirit. One of the wolves was reckless and got too close to Carcajou. It suffered a mangled leg, causing it to flee the scene, dragging a partly severed limb. The companion wolf suddenly lost heart and skulked after its mate. The victor calmly mounted the carcass, looked about defiantly and then commenced to tear away at the innards, gulping great chunks of heart, liver and intestines. The beast was engrossed in its feasting and unaware that an enemy lurked nearby. Olaf stood up ever so silently, raised his rifle to his shoulder, aimed, took a deep breath and gently squeezed the trigger. At the precise moment the bullet had been propelled, the wolverine, with great globs of blood dripping from its jaws, looked around at him and glared defiantly. This brief moment of defiance delayed his chance to escape as the bullet bore into the side of its head, killing it instantly. He was highly pleased to have eradicated his enemy, but, on the other hand, somewhat sorry to have killed such a magnificent beast. Nevertheless, casting aside all feelings of remorse, he skinned the animal on the spot while the flesh was warm and soft. Thor and Kyla were hesitant to approach and sniff at the pelt because it smelled of the dreaded beast. The winter sun slid below the horizon and left them to travel the remaining distance in semi-darkness.

There was rejoicing all around when William finally arrived. The two men greeted each other warmly and the dogs also entered into the excitement of meeting again, frolicking about like children at a nursery. Olaf proudly displayed his wolverine pelt and gave his rendition, a little embellished, about how he got Carcajou. William examined the pelt closely and announced that he was certain it was the same animal that plagued him last winter.

At the crack of dawn, they pulled out for the trading post. During the night, the temperature dipped considerably below zero. The men broke trail for the teams. Since the last storm, the snow on the lake and trail had piled up to depths of four feet in places. They reached Pierre's cabin before dusk and spent a miserable night feeding the fire in between naps. Travelling in the extreme, cold temperature was difficult on the men and dogs. Progress was slow because more stops were required to accommodate the body's need to rest after the laborious plodding. The hazy sun was hovering over the trading post as they pulled into the yard. The men, even though fatigued and frozen through, first, saw to the needs of the dogs before allowing themselves the luxury of the warm store and Ian's Scottish hospitality.

The next two days were busy for the trappers. They purchased groceries, dry goods, hardware, ammunition and other sundries to see them through the rest of the winter. The happy couple, had three full evenings together. They chose August First for the wedding day, the Catholic Church for the ceremony and factor's home for the reception. Olaf discussed his plans to build an extension to the cabin in the spring. He promised that he would be back before the spring break-up to help finalize the plans for the great event. William was honoured to be asked to be the best man, Betty to be bridesmaid and Josie the flower girl. On the last evening, Emma and Ian hosted a celebration party in honour of the happy couple's betrothal.

By the time the travellers had put ten miles behind them, the bottoms of the scattered clouds were tinted a soft yellow by the rising sun. The wind over the last few days had beaten the snow into a hard packed highway, thus making travel fast and effortless. They bypassed Pierre's place and camped in the forest. The men and dogs were comfortably cradled in a spruce lean-to that captured a lot of heat from the crackling fire. It seemed like only minutes had gone by since they fell asleep and the dawning of a new, bright and frosty day. Within a half-hour of waking, the group were gliding along on the lake like two sailing sloops driven before a heavy breeze. The sun was descending below the forest when they arrived at the cabin door. William spent the night and, in the early morning, after a hearty breakfast, his stalwart team whisked him away across the bay. William stated that he and his family would come after break-up for a week and assist in building the extension.

Olaf had been home for several days since completing a successful three-week tour of his trap lines. He had just finished preparing the last pelt when he heard the excited yips of dogs. Upon investigation, he saw Aaron and Moses coming up off the lake with their teams; both men were highly agitated. When they had calmed down, Moses explained that they had come from Hall's Landing where a terrible tragedy had taken place. Special Constable, Joseph One-Shot, had been shot in the chest and left for dead on the trail about two miles from the Trading Post. Though seriously wounded, he struggled the distance to the Police Barracks and related the chilling account about what had happened. He met Bert Bates on the trail heading away from the post. Bert was forced to stop because his sled barred the way. Mary Hunter was securely tied down on Bert's sled. She pleaded to Joseph to make Bert let her go. He demanded that Bert release her immediately and said that he was under arrest for kidnapping. In an animalistic rage, Bert yelled for him to mind his own business as she was his property. When Joseph approached the sled, Bert pulled out a pistol and shot him in the chest and then killed his dogs. A plane was requested from Winepogosis to airlift Joseph to a hospital in Winnipeg, but he succumbed to the wounds before it arrived. Moses added that Joseph was a first cousin and it was their duty, as relatives, to avenge his murder. Sergeant Williams and a group of men from the settlement were heading up to Bert's cabin up Cutter Creek, where he has likely secluded himself. The Sergeant sent Moses and Aaron to fetch Olaf.

Within a short time, the three men and their teams were skimming across the lake on the hard packed snow; the dogs pushed to their limits. Olaf's fearful concerns for Mary and her safety played heavily on his mind. Anger against Bates had built up to such an explosive rage, he wanted to kill him. In four hours, the party reached the entrance to the trail that led to Bert's cabin. There were signs of many dog teams, thus urging them to travel faster. Within the hour they had arrived at the shack. It was snugly nestled in a grove of poplar trees with its back wall pushed up against a steep embankment. Surrounding the cabin, on three sides, were the men from the Post positioned behind trees and rocks; their rifles at the ready and pointing towards the door and windows. Sergeant Williams approached the reinforcements and briefed them on the situation. Bates refuses to lay down his guns and surrender. Since the siege began, Bert had fired several volumes and had wounded one of the men in the shoulder. No return fire had been made thus far because they were concerned about the possibility of hitting Mary. While they stood speaking, several more shots issued from the cabin. A shot lodged itself in a tree just above the sergeant's head.

Throughout the night, four men at a time took the watch in relays, changing every two hours. A relief station was set up in a hollow some distance from the stand-off area. Here, the men were able to warm themselves and have food and warm drinks. The night passed without further occurrence, until just before dawn.

In the silence of the frosty morning, the tired men heard the grating of rusty door hinges. Tensely, they gazed towards the cabin. They watched as it slowly swung open. Sergeant Williams, Olaf, Moses and Aaron were on watch. The Sergeant urgently whispered to the men to hold their fire until the target was in full view. To their astonishment, they saw Mary stumble out the cabin door and scurry like a field mouse over the frozen ground to the safety of the trees. Olaf quickly rose from behind a rock, and, as if shot from a cannon, was at Mary's side and led her to the safety of the camp in the hollow. From within the cabin came the loud clatter of furniture being upturned and scattered, interspersed with loud angry utterances.

Bert suddenly erupted through the gaping door, screaming for Mary to come back. Blood, from an open head wound, trickled into his eyes, momentarily blinding him. Williams hollered for him to put down his rifle and surrender peaceably. Bert wiped the blood from his eyes and stood gaping around him like a stunned bull. His eyes focussed on the scene before him. He roared obscenities at the group and threatened to kill them all. As the group intently watched, Burt visibly transformed from being an angry, belligerent human into a crazed, satanic maniac. With eyes bulging and glaring like those of a depraved beast, he stumbled towards the men, firing his rifle at random in quick succession. The sergeant stood up and yelled for him to put down his rifle and surrender in the name of the law. Bert stared coldly at the sergeant, and, with unbelievable swiftness, shouldered his rifle and aimed directly at Williams. The noise from the rifle resounded throughout the still forest like the rolling thunder of a summer storm. Williams staggered and then collapsed. Bert took aim again but, before he could shoot, Moses stepped out from behind a tree and fatally shot him through the heart; now retribution had been served for the death of his cousin, Joseph. Immediately, Moses and Aaron raced over to where Williams was lying with blood oozing from a head wound, turning the white snow scarlet. His body was motionless and his face was deathly grey, but his shallow breathing indicated that he was still alive. When they gently raised his body to a sitting position, Williams moaned, opened his eyes and stared about in confusion.

The bullet had ploughed a shallow groove across the top of his skull, thus causing him to lose consciousness. Within minutes, the rest appeared on the scene. The sergeant required some first-aid treatment to stem the bleeding. Williams was gingerly helped over to the comfort zone where Mary tended to his wound and placed a temporary bandage round his skull. After his medical attention and several cups of tea, the sergeant looked relaxed in spite of a throbbing pain in his head. Several men returned from checking on Bert and reported that he had probably died instantly. Now that the siege was over, the group gathered around a blazing fire, sipping on mugs of tea, and intently listened while Mary recounted her ordeal.

After lunch on Saturday afternoon, Mary went for a walk through the forest along a well-used trail that skirted the lake. Ahead of her she saw a dog team that was stopped, but no driver was visible. Her curiosity aroused, she proceeded along the trail to where the team was standing; still no driver could be seen. This, she thought, was an odd situation. Suddenly, two powerful arms encircled her from behind and violently wrestled her into the sled and tied her down tightly. She did not know who her assailant was until he threw back his parka-hood and glared into her frightened eyes. She was aghast to see Bert Bates leering down at her, his twisted mouth revealed yellow, rotting teeth and his escaping breath was highly putrid. She opened her mouth wide to scream, but no sound came forth, her throat muscles were constricted due to fear and shock. Bert quickly whipped his team into action and drove them without mercy. Along the trail they encountered Special Constable, Joseph One Shot, who attempted to intervene, but was coldly gunned down along with his dogs. After what seemed a long time, they arrived at the cabin. Bert forcibly hauled her into the cabin and roughly pushed her down onto the bunk and tied her wrists and ankles. Bert was reasonably calm. He talked about his plans for them. He swilled whisky while he paced the floor and expounded on the wonderful life she would have with him. As time passed, he became more inebriated and agitated. Mary sensed that he knew it would not be long before a group from the post will arrive and try to rescue her. Cautiously, she laboured at the rope securing her wrists. It gradually loosened sufficiently to allow her to remove them, but she didn't at this moment.

Several hours had passed when they heard Sergeant Williams holler for Bert to peaceably surrender. Bert became extremely angry at this juncture and savagely roared that he will never give up. In a blind fury, he let off a volley of shots through a broken pane. Since there was no return fire, he settled down and returned to drinking. He had consumed the entire bottle, and then, for the longest time, he sat in his chair, muttering to himself, cursing everyone on earth and vowing to kill all those outside. His big, shaggy head eventually dropped onto the table with a thud and he dozed off. Mary stayed quiet for some time to make certain that he was asleep. With ease, she freed herself from the ropes and stepped slowly and carefully towards the door. Just as she reached the door, her foot bumped against a bucket and the clatter awakened him. Through half-shut, pig-like eyes, he took in the scene and sprang from his chair and lunged at her like an angry bear, but in his drunken stage he tripped over his feet and fell to the floor with a resounding crash. He hit his head sharply against the wood piled by the door. Before he could rise from the floor, Mary forced open the stiff door and nimbly fled for her life.

The sergeant was made comfortable on a sled and Bert's body was loaded onto another. It was mid-afternoon when they arrived back at the post. Several days passed before Williams was well enough to file his report on all that had taken place. Joseph's body was buried in the church cemetery and Bert was buried in a simple grave, adorned with a crude wooden cross, outside the confines of the Catholic cemetery.

Two days after the harrowing ordeal, Olaf and his Indian companions left the landing for their journey home. The three teams travelled together until they reached his cabin. Moses and Aaron spent the night. The morning sky was packed with dark clouds, a stiff, arctic breeze was coming in off the lake and the temperature was well below zero. The two travellers were anxious about the weather and hoped to reach the opening to the home trail before it changed too drastically. Olaf urged them to stay over until the weather cleared, but they were eager to get home to their families and kindly refused the offer. A feeling of anxiety passed through his mind as he waved goodbye to them.

CHAPTER TEN
A TRAGEDY

Later that morning the storm swooped down from the north with surprising suddenness and fury. There was not the usual gentle falling of tiny flakes to indicate or warn of a snowfall. Snow poured from the dark, low lying clouds as if their bellies had been ripped open and the fierce winds, buffeting and pulling with a mighty force, drove the enormous sized flakes into frenzied flurries. Trees were bent by the hurricane like winds and many dead ones were uprooted into windfall piles. The storm viciously pummelled the cabin and it trembled as if a minor earthquake was occurring. When he stepped out to get some firewood, Olaf could not see beyond his extended arm; the land was obliterated in a super whiteout. Olaf figured that he would be snowbound for several days. The storm raged savagely throughout the night and by midday it eventually calmed down to a gentle flutter. He looked out onto a landscape blanketed by a mass, several feet deep, of boring whiteness against the background of a clouded sky with intermittent spots of blue poking through.

On a cloudless and exceptionally frigid day, Olaf and the dogs hit the trail to his trap-line. The blazes on the tree trunks were just as good as signs on a roadway. The snow was deep and he had to break trail for the dogs. After what seemed an eternity, they arrived at Camp One with less than two hours of daylight remaining. He prepared a bivouac at the edge of the trees. After an arduous day of slogging through deep drifts, man and beasts were more than ready to relax in front of a hot, blazing fire and inhale the tantalizing aromas of baked beans, fried bannock and coffee. After four days of gruelling work and subzero temperatures, they headed for home with a fair bundle of furs.

As they were approaching the large beaver pond, the dogs stopped suddenly and stared towards a huge beaver lodge situated in the centre of the pond and growled menacingly. Olaf immediately braced himself for danger and retrieved the rifle from its case. He gently cocked the firing pin and turned his attention to where the dogs were looking. On top of the lodge, he spotted a huge bobcat poised for flight and staring at him with wide open, emotionless eyes. He raised his gun and, before he could shoot, the cat bounded into the safety of the forest. While peering into the forest where the cat had disappeared, he carelessly lowered the cocked rifle, stock down and barrel up, without securing the safety catch. The rifle stock gently clipped the sled runner and, immediately, the sensitive hair trigger released the hammer. He first heard the deafening roar and then felt an excruciating pain ripple along the side of his body. When the initial shock passed, he felt a warm wetness and a throbbing pain. He quickly removed his parka, wool sweater and flannel shirt. The icy air stung his bare torso and he shivered uncontrollably while he examined his wound.

Blood was oozing from a gash just below the rib cage. Fortunately, it was only a shallow flesh wound about five inches long. He applied several handfuls of snow to the wound, which stemmed the flow of blood and relieved the ache. When the bleeding stopped, he cut the sleeves from his shirt and folded them to form a compress. He then cut the remainder of the shirt into strips, knotted the ends together and then tied the crude bandage around his body so as to snugly hold the compress in place. While he was doctoring himself, his body trembled and his teeth chattered like a pair of castanets. He hurriedly donned his wool sweater and parka and continued homeward. During the journey home, Olaf reflected on how precarious a trapper's existence is and that the pendulum of life could stop swinging at any moment. In a few weeks, the wound had sufficiently healed without complications but a perpetual scar will remain as a memento of his carelessness.

The sun lingered several minutes longer each day, a sign that spring was on its way. Now, he thought, would be a good time to take advantage of the extended daylight and do some hunting. They started out on a cloudless and windless day, crossed the Grass River and travelled in a westerly direction. Two hours into the morning, they came upon a well-travelled game trail that snaked its way through an area of dense scrub growth. Judging by the width and hardness of the trail, Olaf conjectured that this was the regular route of a moose herd whose winter yard-up area must be close by. They had not travelled far when a startled moose, secluded from view by small pine trees and a thick growth of shrubs, quickly arose from its lying down position and casually loped off down the trail. It did not travel far when it stopped and curiously stared at the intruders. This was its downfall. A well-placed shot brought the beast down. It was a two-year-old bull and looked to be in good health in spite of the harsh winter. From the bountiful carcass he retrieved the front and hind quarters, brisket, liver, heart and fat for rendering. Olaf had to assist the dogs to pull the sled to get the enormous load to the cabin.

Now that the meat larder was sufficiently stocked, a four day trip was made to the line camps. They returned from the tour with the best catch of the season thus far. He piled the frozen carcasses against the wall, furthest away from the stove, to allow them to gradually thaw before he could skin them. Over the next two days, while the hides were softening, he scouted the woods behind his cabin and selected straight, stout pine trees to be felled for building the extension. Each tree selected had a wide slash chiselled into the bark, identifying it for the axe. He figured that there was a week's work to cut, trim and debark the trees and skid them out to the cabin before the snow gets too soft.

March blew in like the proverbial lion, flexing its muscles, with squalls of freezing snow swooping down from the arctic regions. It was because of one of these out of the blue storms that Olaf's life was put in jeopardy due to a rash decision. He was on his trap line and because the weather was amenable, he completed his work in record time. While at Camp Three, on an impulse, he decided to make a trip to Fox Lake to visit with Chief Anokee and his people. He figured to travel in a north-westerly direction and, within two to three hours, should pick up the trail to the reserve. In the early morning chill, he confidently struck out, unconcerned that he was entering unfamiliar territory. Olaf used the rising sun as a directional guide.

Everything was going well as they gobbled up the miles through an area of wide spread, stunted pines. Soon they came to a large expanse of frozen marsh that extended to the edge of the distant forest. Olaf was anxious to get to the trees because to the north he could see dark storm clouds swelling and rapidly filling the sky like a tidal wave. Within minutes the blue sky transformed into a sea of black clouds scudding across the sky like waves pounding towards a distant shore. An eerie duskiness swept across the land, a stiff breeze tugged savagely at them and heavy flakes of snow crowded out all landmarks. The arctic wind intensified and the freezing snow battered them viciously. He had no sense of direction and deeply feared that they might wander about aimlessly in circles. They staggered about, enveloped in a shroud of solid white. He lunged ahead of the dogs, shouting words of encouragement. Several times they stopped to rest and regain their breath. Their dire predicament seemed endless. Progress was slow; each step forward became more arduous, as if his feet were tied to lead weights.

Olaf plodded along in a state of confusion; several times he stumbled and fell to his knees. Each time, it took longer to get up. It felt so comfortable to lie where he fell, but the insidious cold pierced his clothing and bit into his flesh like so many tiny daggers, forcing him to rise and forge ahead. Eventually, after a lengthy time of senseless roaming, he collapsed and lay in a motionless heap, the forerunner to death by freezing. His body eventually became oblivious to the cold and he felt at peace; his mind hallucinated about his childhood and family; his spirit was ready to be lifted from his body. While his mind drifted from the conscious to the unconscious, an incessant, sharp noise penetrated his mind and he felt a warm moistness spread over his face. With much difficulty, he slowly opened his eyes and peered ahead as if looking through a fog.

After several dazed moments, his tired eyes became focused and there, in front of his face, were Thor and Kyla, jumping about excitedly, barking and licking him. They kept bouncing back and forth as if they were trying to tell him something. Slowly and painfully he struggled on to his hands and knees and laboriously crawled after them, the snowshoes dangling behind with the harness around his ankles. The forced movement increased the circulation throughout his body. The relentless wind and snow continued to lash at them, thus their progress was slow and exhausting. Suddenly, as if by magic, the storm seemed less severe and the snow was not so deep.

He realized that he was amidst trees. The dogs had led him from a certain death on the marsh into the safety of the forest where the savage storm did not have the same harshness. After several long minutes, Olaf felt some strength creep into his body. He freed himself of the snowshoes, stiffly arose, flailed his arms about and chicken hopped on the spot. This activity limbered his stiff muscles and returned some heat to his body. He donned the snowshoes and led the dogs further into the forest. They plodded along in the dim light, taking the easiest route to avoid the treacherous deadfalls. The terrain dropped off into a dried creek bed and on the opposite bank there was an overhang of dead trees jutting halfway across. The bank, below the deadfalls, was hollowed out due to water erosion of years gone-by and provided an ideal shelter from the storm. His first concern was to get a fire going. With painful fingers, stiff from the extreme cold, he struggled to unhitch the dogs and haul the sled into the shelter. In frantic desperation, with leaden hands, he fumbled through the pack for the fire starters, chunks of kindling finely sliced and easily ignited. Around these he stacked slender, dried branches to form a tipi which would form the base for adding larger sticks as needed.

After five desperate tries, the fire made a weak attempt to burn and, with delicate pampering, he finally coaxed the flames to come to life. He passionately hugged both dogs and thanked them for saving his life. After their meal of moose jerky and hard tack biscuits, they slept the sleep of the dead while the storm raged throughout the long night. Olaf was awakened by the raucous cries of the ravens that were perched in the treetops directly above him. He blinked several times to focus on the winter wonderland before him. The storm had blown itself out and shafts of daylight were filtering through the branches. The world was at peace again. He renewed the fire by feeding the glowing embers dead twigs and branches that were eagerly gobbled by the greedy flames.

Olaf brewed a pail of tea to wash down the jerky and biscuits. Daylight penetrated the dusky dimness of the forest; it was time to for them to go. They worked their way back to the marsh and continued the journey to Fox

Lake. Within the hour, they had left the frozen, tundra like marsh and skirted the forest through several miles of stunted pine. Frost crystals hung over the landscape like a pall from a distant forest fire. By midmorning, the barely warm rays of the sun, struggling to break through the cloud cover, had burned off most of the icy haze. Their exhaled breath momentarily hung over their heads like miniature clouds. At midday they come across a well used trail that led along the edge of a bench-land that overlooked a tear-drop shaped lake, which Olaf surmised to be Fox Lake. From this vantage point, he could see a cluster of log cabins dotted about the clearing along the shoreline. One large building, which he figured was the community hall, sat aloof at the far end of the settlement as if holding court over the lesser buildings. Swelling puffs of white smoke from black metal chimneys wafted upwards into the frosty air. Close to each cabin, he could see small groups of sled dogs curled up in circular heaps, trying to maximize their own body warmth. Otherwise, there was no other sign of life.

They proceeded along the trail that wound its way through the trees down a gentle slope to the edge of the settlement. Before they even reached the clearing, every dog in the settlement joined in a chorus of howls and barking, alerting the people inside. Olaf was relieved to see that the reserve dogs were tethered to individual posts, thus restraining them from attacking Thor and

Kyla. Immediately, doors were flung open and heads popped out like figures from Jack-in-the-boxes. At the first cabin he asked where the Chief's cabin was situated. In pigeon English, an elderly man directed him to a lone cabin situated at the far end of the clearing. The chief was standing in the doorway when Olaf pulled up to the shack and when he recognized who the stranger was, his eyes grew large with surprise, his mouth widened into a smile and he quietly chortled. After salutations were exchanged, Olaf tended to the dogs before going inside. He was introduced to the chief's wife, Anyiato, a plump woman with coal-black, shiny hair tidily pulled back to reveal a round, pleasant face with large, twinkling brown eyes. Over copious cups of strong tea, bannock and roast moose, the chief and Olaf quietly discussed their individual events that occurred since they last saw each other. Anyiato was ever in the background seeing to their needs.

Olaf inquired about Moses and Aaron and their journey from his place on the day the storm struck. Immediately, Anokee's countenance changed from happiness to that of deep sadness. He cleared his throat and wiped away tears that had welled up in the corners of his eyes. Anyiato's head dropped to her chest and she stifled a loud sob and her whole body trembled. He stared at his hosts. Immediately, his thoughts went back to the day Moses and Aaron left his home and his sense of nervous anxiety. With a heavy feeling of dread, he hesitantly asked in a choked voice what was wrong. The chief composed himself and in a grievous tone said that they were dead; frozen to death. Olaf was stunned and felt as if his heart had stopped. The Chief's voice quivered as he emotionally related the sad story. The second day after the blizzard, the eight dogs appeared at the village without the sleds and drivers. Fearing the worst, he sent out a search party to find them. The searchers returned after twelve hours with the bodies of Moses and Aaron. They were found on the trail, at the edge of the forest, under a mound of snow huddled together as if trying to keep each other warm. The sleds were turned on their sides and at their backs to act as wind barriers. Apparently they became disorientated in the wind and snow and chose to stop to wait out the storm. They had un-harnessed the dogs so they could fend for themselves and seek their own shelter. Sometime during that fateful storm, they entered into the realms of the never-ending sleep. He ended by stating that the "Storm Spirit" called for their souls to enter into the great land in the sky. Olaf was devastated and inwardly grieved the loss of his two friends. He blamed himself for not successfully convincing them to abandon their plans to leave.

A heavy stillness and an air of sadness permeated the cabin. After some uncomfortable moments, he expressed his sorrow and sympathy. He told them about the events that took place at Bate's cabin, their staying overnight and declining to remain another night. They thankfully accepted the condolences and said that, if he wanted, he could see them in the storage shed behind the main hall. They had been placed there until the police came to make out a death report and also to await the warmer weather when their graves could be prepared. The old chief donned his Hudson's Bay parka and mukluks and led the way to the storage shed. The old man, stooped and slow from aging, shuffled ahead. The grey, weathered plank door hung askew on two rusty, tired hinges. Inside the small room, the air was extremely frigid and it was dimly lit by shafts of sunlight poking through the open door. Vapours of breath puffed from the two men as they gazed at the frozen corpses set in the foetal position and arms crossed over their hearts. Olaf was bewildered as to how this could have happened to two men who lived their entire lives in the wilds and were highly knowledgeable in bush lore. Droplets of tears trickled onto his cheeks and immediately turned to ice. With a choked throat, he whispered farewell to his friends and then stumbled out into the glaring light of the afternoon.

In Olaf's honour, the chief called for a powwow. The entire population, youngest to the oldest, gathered in the community hall. Members, who weren't self conscious, enjoyed telling stories of the past and about their adventurous exploits. Those who were physically able shuffled around in a huge circle to the beat of a drum. Bannock, grease bread and tea were served from a long, log table during the entire evening. On two occasions, Olaf was dragged into the dance circle where he tripped and two stepped his way to the amusement of the dancers as well as the onlookers. Well into the early hours of the morning, the chief stood and loudly called for everyone's attention. He motioned for all to be seated. From the corner of the hall a short, grizzled, old, hump-backed individual, Totono, the Medicine man, one leg shorter than the other, limped over and stood next to the chief.

The chief spoke at great length about how Olaf showed kindness and respect to himself and his sons and how he accepted the Fox Lake people with humility and never showed arrogance to any of them. He concluded by stating that Olaf will now be made an honorary member of the Fox Lake Band. The chief raised his feathered staff above his head and the people stood and cheered. The honoured guest was beckoned by the chief to come and stand next to him. When the cheering ceased, Totono stood to his fullest and in a monotonous, singsong voice expounded philosophically about love, honour and truth amongst one another. He then approached Olaf and gently touched his crown with an ornate ceremonial staff covered with bleached, beaded moose hide, and loudly proclaimed him to be called "Gentle Spirit". Anyiato presented Olaf with a white tanned moose hide jacket decorated with minute glass beads. Olaf then spoke to the assembly and expressed how proud he felt to be honoured by such a memorable bestowal and that his heart was filled with the greatest of joy.

The temperature hovered at thirty below on the morning he left Fox Lake. Every member of the community cheered him on as he sped by their homes and up the slope to the main trail. Due to the bitter cold of the early morning, frequent stops were made to rest and gain their wind. On the way he was able to view the landscape through which he passed previously on that nearly fatal, stormy day. It took four days to clear and reset his traps. They arrived home during the late afternoon on the fifth day, just ahead of the snow that had threatened to fall since they left Camp One that morning.

The snow fell heavily for two days, confining them to the cabin, so he took advantage of this to prepare his pelts and put his culinary skills to use. The warm cabin was full of mouth watering aromas of fresh baked bread, bannock and simmering moose stew that intermingled with the strong odours of freshly stretched hides. After a week at home, he made a journey around his trap lines and gathered up a very worthwhile pile of furs. The weather conditions were ideal; azure skies, crispy, invigorating temperatures and no wind. He noticed a gradual change in the climate; temperatures were warmer more often than not. He noticed that the snow cover on the beaver ponds was changing from white to grey-blue, a good indication that the ponds will be free of ice in a few weeks. When that happens, he will turn his attention to trapping beavers.

On a fine morning at the end of March, Jim Barnes made his last, winter visit before the ice went out. He manoeuvred the plane around several pressure cracks while taxiing towards the landing. The friends had a lengthy visit. Olaf recounted all that happened since he last saw him. He told Jim of his betrothal to Mary and extended him a invitation to the wedding. Jim promised he would make every effort to attend. Jim was to fly several bundles of Olaf's fur to the Hall's Landing. Olaf hastily wrote a letter to Mary, bringing her up to date. It was two o'clock when Jim jockeyed his way through the ice mounds to reach the open area for a clean take-off.

CHAPTER ELEVEN

TRAGIC DISCOVERY

The sun was rising earlier and setting later each day and the snow on the trails and the ice on the lake were beginning to deteriorate. Now was a good time to bring in the trees for the cabin extension. He downed all the selected trees, lopped their branches, debarked and sawed them into the proper lengths. With help from the dogs, the logs were skidded out to the cabin and stacked off the ground on a frame support. Now it was up to Mother Nature to cure the logs over the next few months.

It was mid April when the Grass River broke through its covering of ice. It flowed in full spate and carried debris, along with large chunks of ice, out into the lake. The noise, from the powerful force of the rushing water churning up forest debris and ice, sounded like a freight train rumbling down the tracks. The centre of the lake had opened and was mostly free of ice but the ice from the shore out to the open water was rotting and lay under a foot of water.

It took him a month to shutdown his trapping and close up the line camps. The ponds were prolific with prime beavers. He was successful in making a catch of forty pelts, the majority being the larger or blanket pelts. As a change of diet, he roasted a fat beaver carcass, stuffed with seasoned, crumbled bannock and rice. The fat drippings made excellent tasting gravy. The meat was succulent and sweet.

At the end of May, the lake was bare of all ice, except for the tenacious slush that dominated most of the shoreline. He decided that in a couple of days he should make a trip to Hall's Landing, but, in the meantime, he had to clean up and put away the traps and do some touch up repairs to the canoe. Now that Mary will be part of his life, he will have to purchase a larger canoe.

The lakes, bays and shallows were alive with flocks of geese and ducks that stopped off to feed on their way north. The loons were back, filling the air with their silly, laughter like cries. It was pleasant to have the colourful summer birds flitting about and chirping melodiously; a more pleasant contrast to the raucous blackbirds and magpies that lingered all winter. The poplar and hardwood trees were bursting forth with new, green growth and the wild flowers were popping up like mushrooms. Spring brought a new vitality to the land. It filled him with a renewed vigour and he looked forward to his second year as a trapper.

Shoulder muscles rippled under his shirt as he deftly propelled the canoe across the crystal, clear water. It was wonderful to be on the water again. The dogs stood, with front paws on the thwart, looking eagerly ahead with their noses in the air, sniffing at the gentle breeze. They had a mug-up and sandwich in a cosy bay with a crescent shaped white, sandy beach. Thor and Kyla took advantage of the stopover and happily explored every inch of the area. Olaf was just finishing his sandwich when the dogs let out a chorus of excited barks. He went over to where they were standing and he spotted a fawn lying in the tall grass. It was trying its best to appear as an inanimate object, but its trembling, little frame and blinking, sorrowful, brown eyes belied this possibility. He observed the doe a little ways off amongst the trees. It was pacing back and forth, somewhat distressed. It wanted to come to her baby's rescue, but was too timid to face the dogs. He called the dogs off and returned to the canoe. As they pushed off, he saw her hesitantly edge her way back to her baby. He waved his paddle as a salute to Pierre's old cabin when they glided past. In the late afternoon he swung eastward across the bottom of the lake and headed for the landing about twenty minutes away. There was the usual greeting from howling dogs and Indian children gathering on the dock.

Ian, wearing a wide, happy grin on his swarthy face, sprinted down to the landing and greeted him.

They shook hands vigorously and slapped each others shoulder and laughed loudly. Mary was so overjoyed to see Olaf that she squealed with delight and immediately flung her arms around him. They embraced and kissed passionately. Emma and Ian chuckled at this affectionate display. After supper, the young couple took a long, casual stroll along the lakeshore with the dogs in tow. Mary stated that her family will be coming for the wedding and all the arrangements were in place for the church, reception dinner and evening party. He informed her that Betty Watson was very honoured to be her bridesmaid and Josie the flower girl. Mary stated that she was eager to meet them.

During the evening, while having tea and cakes, Olaf talked about Moses and Aaron and mentioned that the tribe bestowed on him the name of "Gentle Spirit". All were devastated over the tragedy. Ian said that there had been no members from the Fox Lake since the Bate's situation and he had often wondered why. On the other hand, all were pleased about his honoured name. He was hesitant to tell about his near fatal accident due to the careless handling of the rifle, but when he did, Mary's face registered shock. It frightened her that he could lose his life so easily. She begged him to be ultra careful. Ian shook his head as If to say that Olaf was lucky this time but that may not always be the case. To prevent Mary further anxiety, Ian did not verbalize that during his time as a factor, several trappers had been accidentally killed and others have never been found; their disappearances are still a mystery to this day. To spare Mary additional concern, Olaf did not mention about him being a victim of nearly freezing to death. When he was leaving to go to his quarters, Mary hugged him tightly and made him promise to be very cautious.

The canoe was heavily loaded with store-bought supplies, thus leaving the dogs without the freedom to move about, so they curled up on top of the load and snoozed. They moved along the east shore for a change. A slight breeze created wavelets that rhythmically slapped the canoe's prow and the brilliant sun rays playfully reflected off the surface, causing Olaf to squint. As far as his eyes could see, the land was bathed in lush green. The shoreline was rugged and rocky, interspersed with pristine beaches. Ahead he spotted a picturesque, sandy cove with a small stream tumbling into the lake. They stopped there to have lunch and a rest. While waiting for the tea pail to come to a boil, Olaf casually scouted around. He discovered a very old, densely overgrown trail that led off into the forest. After he had eaten, he explored the trail a little ways. There was an eerie stillness within the dim forest. Tangled undergrowth made it difficult to discern where the trail had once existed. The blaze marks were mere scars from days long past. After about fifteen minutes he emerged into an area, that had once been a clearing, crowded out by years of over-growth and there, before him, stood a very old, weathered log cabin. The roof was sagging in the centre and partly collapsed at one corner where the chimney once protruded. The walls were in varying stages of collapse; the crumbling, grey logs were fragile and filled with powdered pulp. The windows and door were nothing more than black holes staring forlornly into the forest. A huge pine tree and several smaller poplars grew from inside the cabin and poked their leafy limbs through the roof. Olaf surmised that the age of this sorry sight was well over thirty years. He peered inside through a gaping window. It took a few moments for his eyes to become accustomed to the dimness; what light there was came from the hole in the roof. His eyes darted about the small room as if they were on a swivel. He quickly returned his gaze to a part of the cabin he had just viewed. What he saw through the hazy sunrays made his heart almost stop, for there in the corner, on a bunk bed, was a clothed skeleton with a rusted rifle across its chest. On the floor, near the bunk, was another skeleton in a sitting position, leaning against the wall. At first, he did not believe what he was seeing

He carefully picked his way through the chaos of debris, upturned furniture and stove. It was apparent that some sort of scuffle had occurred. The jacket of the skeleton on the floor had a large hole over the region of the heart. The one on the bunk, with its skull and jaws blown away, had a note clutched in its fleshless hand. Olaf gently pried the note from its grasp. He had to be careful, as the paper was beginning to disintegrate. The note, barely legible, printed with an uneducated hand, read, "Jan 11, 1890, I kilt my buddy cause he was making me crasey. I cood not stand any more, so I shot him. God bless him and forgive me. LouisAndres". It appeared to be a case of two people living in cramped quarters, without personal space, under harsh conditions and having to deal with individual frustrations on a daily basis. The trappers' term for this is "gone shack wacky", when a person's mind snaps. This sad tragedy is but one of many that occur within the harsh confines of an isolated environment, where only the strong in spirit and fortitude can survive. He left everything as he found it. He guessed that reporting his find to Sergeant Williams on his next visit to the post will be time enough, after all what will another month matter to Lee's investigation. On the way out he blazed the trail and, at the beach, he erected a stone cairn to aid the sergeant in locating the site.

It took Olaf the better part of a week to clear the area where the extension was to be built and to gather enough field rocks for the fireplace. Collecting the rocks was an arduous chore. He would scout the shore line and load suitable rocks into the canoe and haul them up the path to the cabin. Close by, up the Grass River, he located a source of clay soil which he lugged back to the cabin in buckets. Everything was now ready for when the Watsons arrive to assist him to enlarge the cabin.

That evening, before retiring, Olaf wrote a letter to his family and one to Stefan. Also, he compiled a list of articles and supplies for Jim to bring from Winnipeg. The order consisted of a double bed with spring mattress, bedding, blankets, a heavy duty cook stove, dishes, cutlery, pots, pans, nails, roofing paper, heavy glass windows, a factory made door and a host of other necessary items. Satisfied with his efforts, he sat back and puffed on old faithful and exclaimed to the dogs, who perked their ears, that time can now slip by in a hurry, the sooner the better.

CHAPTER TWELVE
THE ANNEX

Early in June Olaf headed out for Camp One. The day was balmy and a gentle breeze caressed his face and bare arms. The dogs, settled on top of the load, scanned the view before them and with eager noses inhaled the strange odours that emanated from every direction. Two hours of steady paddling brought them to a sandy beach, the point from which they would head inland to Camp One. He stowed the canoe alongside a heavy growth of thickets several yards from the water's edge. Without having to hoist it directly from ground level, he placed the backpack on a tall rock and backed into the harness. With the heavy pack strapped on and both hands encumbered with tools, he set off on the trail. The dogs ranged throughout the forest, but never too far from Olaf's sight. Along the way, he saw fresh bear scats. This concerned him because more than likely they would be from an adult bear with cubs. He called his dogs and ordered them to heel. The last thing he needed was for Thor and Kylie to become involved with the cubs and rile the mother. He did not want to be forced to shoot the angry sow and leave the babies motherless. They finally reached the camp without any problems.

To clear the site and cut the logs for the new camp took up most of what was left of the afternoon. By late evening of the next day, a cosy, roomy line camp had been completed. That night he put the rustic abode to the test. The bed, a log platform that rested about ten inches off the ground and covered with a mattress of spruce boughs, proved to be reasonably comfortable. A narrow shelf attached to the wall, was used as an eating and work area. Before the next trapping season, he planned to install a sheet metal stove. Prior to leaving the camp, he cut and split a huge pile of wood for the coming winter.

They arrived at the lake during the early afternoon and his first action was to build a fire over which he hung the tea pail. On an impulse, while waiting for the tea water to come to a boil, he stripped and plunged into the chilly water and frolicked about like a child in a swimming pool. The dogs sat on the shore and gazed at him with perplexed looks because they have never seen him behave like this. He tried to coax them to join in but they backed away and looked at him as if they doubted his sanity. After ten minutes of splashing and diving, he clambered out and playfully chased the dogs. They immediately accepted this sudden caper as a game and joined in the fun, barking and jumping about like silly children. The water was on the boil, so he quickly dressed and prepared lunch.

As the canoe glided up to the landing, the late afternoon light was being replaced by the greyness of dusk. By the time the canoe was unloaded and the gear stored away, the grey light turned to black. At lights out, the sough of soft breezes through the pines and the gentle, rhythmic slapping of small waves against the rocky shore was all that he could hear. He muttered to himself that something must be blowing in from the north. During the night, he was awakened by the brilliant, flash of lightening and the deafening thunder clap that followed. The lashing rain beat heavily on the shingles and the angry waves savagely pounded against the land. The rain and windstorm storm attacked with a frenzy and demonically hurled themselves at everything on the land. By early dawn the fury of the storm had abated but a steady drizzle continued to drench the landscape. Today, Olaf thought, will be a stay-in day to get on with household tasks and baking. The dogs were curled up at the foot of the glowing stove, sound asleep, oblivious of what was happening outside.

Olaf was kneading bread dough when both dogs suddenly stood up and, with low-throated growls, ran to the door. Rubbing off the excess flour and dough, he strode to the door and yanked it open. Thor and Kyla flew through the opening with lightning speed and raced behind the cabin, frantically yipping. The dogs didn't respond to his calls and whistles to return. Within minutes a deafening ruction broke out from within the forest. A chorus of barks mixed with the deep throated growls and snarls from a bear filled the air. His worst fear was that the dogs were confronting a sow and her young. Without hesitation, he ran to the cabin and returned with a loaded rifle and hurriedly made his way towards the commotion. In a clearing, he saw Thor and Kyla harassing a young black bear. It was standing in a defensive position, menacingly waving its arms with claws extended, ready to do harm should it be attacked. Olaf sized up the situation and he realized that the bear, about a two year-old, did not have its heart in a full scale battle; it just wanted to be left alone. He whistled to the dogs and ordered them to his side. With reluctance they obeyed and this gave the beast a chance to climb a sturdy pine tree. Having had their bit of sport, the dogs were now contented to return home with their master. During the afternoon the drizzle ceased as abruptly as a shower being turned off. The black clouds were quickly dispersed by the lofty breezes and signs of heavy moisture permeated the land all around. The numerous formed puddles, pools and swollen back-waters will now become breeding grounds for the highly hated, blood-sucking mosquitoes.

Several days after the storm, they set out by canoe to visit the post. The sun was at its apex when he spotted smoke billowing lazily across the lake. He guessed that it was coming from a small sandy cove on the other side of the low-lying rocky, spit just ahead. When he rounded the point he saw two men sitting on a drift-wood log. They were deeply engrossed in conversation and eating, thus unaware of the canoe. As he came nearer, Olaf called out the bush-man's ahoy, to alert them that he was approaching. The men turned and stood up to view the unexpected visitor. Their brown faces beamed when they recognized who it was. The men, from the Fox Lake Reserve, were the nephews of the Chief. Friendly greetings were exchanged, and Gerald, the older of the two, extended an invitation to join them at their meal. Tommy stirred up the glowing coals over which he placed a split trout on a forked branch. The Indians were on their return journey from the trading post. They stated that all was well and quiet at the landing. Gerald spoke about Chief Anokee's failing health and said that he had been elected by the people to be chief when the old man passes away. His health had been falling rapidly, so he called a pre-election to have the new chief ready upon his demise. Olaf expressed his concern and sorrow and asked that they inform the chief that he will visit him shortly after he returns from the post. After an hour of visiting, they parted company. Several hours of paddling brought them to the landing. The usual dogs' choruses and laughing children greeted him. Soon the entire village was alerted to his arrival.

He visited for three days, during which, he and Mary finalized their wedding plans. The days were blissful for the couple. They discussed and re-discussed their plans for the future. Alas, the time for departure had come too quickly. He could not spare more time because the Watsons were expected within a few days to assist in the building of the extension. The sun had barely risen when he pulled away from the dock. A heavy mist from the lake quickly enveloped the travellers as if a ghostly shroud had dropped over them. Clutching at her coat with one hand, Mary stood on the shore looking like a forlorn orphan as tears slowly edged their way down her cheeks. A loon's eerie cry floated from across the lake, making her feel more lonesome.

Olaf had been home for three days before William and his family arrived. Betty and Josie were assigned to the household duties of cooking, cleaning and washing, as well as entertaining the dogs. Also, as if he had planned the opportune time to deliver the goods and wares, Jim arrived the following day. After the aircraft left, the goods were transferred from the beach to the cabin.

Three weeks of steady, concerted effort resulted in the completion of the extension. The addition was attached to the west end of the main cabin which was now transformed into a tee-shaped structure. Inside, it was divided into two large rooms, a separate bedroom and living-room, both relying on the fire-place and kitchen range for warmth. One end of the living-room was partitioned off to accommodate a spacious storage-room. The cooking range and new bed were set in place. One large window allowed daylight to enter the living-room and a door led to the outside. An additional feature, not previously planned, was incorporated into the building process. A roofed porch, with front and side rails, was erected at the main entrance to the cabin. It was large enough for a bench and a chair. Betty was impressed with the cabin's cosiness and indicated that Mary will be very pleased with her new home.

William and his family took their leave and promised to return two days before the wedding. Jim, on his recent visit offered to pick up the group, dogs as well, at Olaf's cabin and fly them to the landing on the day before the wedding and bring them back the next day after the ceremonies.

For the next three weeks Olaf busied himself finishing off the cabin interior. He built new shelving in the storage room, new pine-log kitchen table and chairs, shelves in the kitchen, bed-side table and wash-stand. He cleared the outside area of overgrowth, tidied the wood pile and made a bench with a back and armrests so they could sit on the porch and enjoy the view across the lake.

CHAPTER THIRTEEN
THE PASSING OF A CHIEF

Olaf had done all that was needed to make the cabin comfortable for his bride to-be. As there was a space of four weeks between now and the wedding day, he decided that it would be a good time to visit the Fox Lake Reserve. Late June and early July were very hot and dry; there hadn't been a decent rain since the last severe storm in May. As he paddled along the lakeshore he saw that the vegetation was withered and lacked the lustre of healthy summer foliage. The sun was relentless as it shone down upon the earth. The temperature was in the high eighties and not a wisp of a breeze blew to give any respite from the heat. They reached the trail head at high noon and stored the canoe under cover of a thicket growing beyond the beach. Before they tackled the trail to the reserve, man and beasts revelled in the refreshing water, jumping about in wild excitement. Fully rejuvenated, the trio set off on the dusty, well trodden trail.

The afternoon heat was unbearable and by the time the trio arrived at the bench overlooking the Indian village, Olaf's clothing was drenched with perspiration and the dogs were panting rapidly. The settlement dogs were tethered in the shade behind their owners' shacks, lying flat-out. Some had laboriously raised their heads to stare as they passed but made no effort to stand or bark. Without the canine hubbub, the villagers, secluded in their homes to escape the heat, were unaware of their arrival so they made their way to Anokee's cabin unobserved.

The door was wide open and he could see Anyiato sitting by the bed upon which Anokee was lying, slightly propped up on rope backrest. His eyes were shut and his breathing was laboured and shallow, low rasping sounds emanated from his gaping mouth. A gentle tap alerted Anyiato to another's presence and when she recognized Olaf, she rose to greet him with tears trickling down her brown cheeks and there was deep sadness in her eyes. It appeared that she has been in this state of sorrow and anxiety for some time. Tightly grasping his hands she emotionally uttered, in Cree, how kind it was that "Gentle Spirit" came to see the great chief who will be so pleased to see him again. With a choked-up throat and tears welling up in his eyes, Olaf spoke to her quietly and gently stroked her black hair to soothe her troubled state. The desired effect was achieved, she seemed more at ease while she held his hands. Quietly they stepped to the bed and sadly looked down at the dying man. In the dim light, he could make out the pallid, wasted body of a man who once was, as he remembered, the epitome of one who had a zest for life. His heart felt tightly twisted within his chest and tears flowed freely from his hot, blinking eyes as he watched his friend lay, slowly dying before his eyes.

In her Pigeon English, Anyiato informed him that the chief had taken ill last winter and had not fully recovered. His illness, which Olaf surmised must have been the flu, weakened him greatly and what with fevers and harsh coughing his health deteriorated rapidly. He refused to leave the reserve to attend a hospital in the south for fear of dying in a strange place away from his beloved family and people. The stillness of the cabin was broken by faint mumbles coming from the chief. His glassy eyes were wide open and a faint smile struggled to his lips when he gazed upon Olaf. They rushed to his side. He struggled to whisper that he was very pleased to see his good friend. Anyiato and Olaf sat on opposite sides of the bed, each holding a cold, skinny hand. These few moments with his wife and friend gave Anokee a boost. He glanced back and forth at the two of them with a faint sparkle in his eyes and then, with a weak squeeze from his hands, he closed his eyes and the two felt his life ebb from his emaciated body; he was gone. Anyiato laid her head on the bed an openly wailed with grief. Olaf felt deep sorrow build up inside him and he sobbed as though it were his own father who had died.

As if by some silent, secret communication system, the chief's demise was known to the members of the tribe and soon a crowd of mourners gathered outside the cabin. The men, stony faced, stood with bowed heads while the women rocked back and forth emitting soul-penetrating wails interspersed by uncontrollable sobs. The reserve dogs picked up the cue and all joined-in with their plaintive, canine howls. En masse they communicated the sad news throughout the forest and across the lake.

The next day, Anokee's body was ceremoniously placed on display in the community hall for the community to pay their last respects. Totono, the Medicine Man, presided over the sad gathering with prayers and tales of Anokee's greatness in life. Then the chief's frail body, dressed in his finest chieftain's garb along with his prized earthly possessions, was placed into a rustic, pine board coffin. The long procession, headed by Anyiato and his immediate relatives, slowly proceeded to the cemetery, located in a shady grove of popular trees at the far end of the village. Muffled sounds of grief prevailed during the slow walk to the burial ground. The crowd bunched around the white picket fence and watched as their beloved leader's remains were slowly lowered into its final resting place. All this time, Olaf stood as a spectator who did not wish to intrude on the people's private moments of grief.

Following the burial ceremony, the village congregated at the community hall to partake in a feast honouring Anokee. Gerald personally invited Olaf to share their food. He was seated at the head table with, Gerald, the new chief, the council members, Anyiato and Totono. During the gathering, the new chief spoke about Anokee's many achievements as their leader and how he, himself, will strive to serve the tribe well. Following, each council member, in turn, rose and eloquently honoured their past chief. Gerald then invited "Gentle Spirit" to speak to the assembly. Olaf's reverent words were interpreted to the people through Gerald. The Medicine Man performed the ritual of swearing-in the new chief and council and pronounced the blessings of the spirits upon them. The day's events were concluded with drum dancing and chanting which carried on well into the night.

Saying farewell this time was on a sombre note. He promised to visit next fall, and bring his wife. His statement caused a chuckle amongst the villagers and they clapped their approval. Gerald told Olaf that Anokee had wanted to attend his wedding, but when he realized his illness would prevent this, he asked him to go and represent his people if it was agreeable to "Gentle Spirit". Olaf replied that he and his bride would be greatly honoured to have him and any others who wished to attend. The morning sun was a fire-ball, radiating waves of scorching heat, when he departed.

CHAPTER FOURTEEN
FOREST FIRE

In spite of the intense heat, they arrived at the lake in record time. While enjoying a brief respite with a mug of tea and hard-tack, Olaf detected a faint odour of wood smoke and noticed that the sun struggled to shine through a translucent sky. The breezes aloft were propelling clouds of ochre coloured smoke through the ever darkening sky. Apprehensive about this, he quickly terminated his lunch. The further south they travelled, greater was the amount of dark smoke filling the sky and stronger was the smell of burning wood. Without a doubt, a forest-fire was in progress. His heart pounded like a jack-hammer against his chest walls and he feared the worst. It was not long before he could see the flames leaping from tree to tree; it was a crown fire. Breathing became more difficult and his eyes were smarting and watering. The frightened dogs shivered nervously, whined fearfully and sneezed constantly. From his vantage point he surmised that the fire was creeping its way north westerly, away from his home area, but was within the region of the Watson's place. Without further delay he dug his paddle into the water and his arms were pistons propelling the craft up the bay. Olaf saw flames galloping through the forest as they fed on the sap filled pines and the rapid movement of overheated air, sounded like a distant, rumbling, freight train, rushing in to replace the cool air that was dispersed by the intense heat. Trees were exploding from the pressures of expanding resin gases and blazing chunks of wood and bark hurtled haphazardly through the air seeking new targets to ignite. All along the rocky shore the bone-dry vegetation was gobbled up by the crackling flames as if they were sharks on a feeding frenzy. They gasped and choked from gulping in amounts of the smoke, tainted air. They huddled low in the canoe to take advantage of the drafts of cool air sucked into the bay from the lake. Although paddling was hampered, Olaf was able to creep steadily towards Watson's beach.

Squinting through the haze, he saw William, standing on a ladder, throwing water on to the shingled roof from buckets that Betty handed up to him. On the beach, Josie was filling two buckets which Mary rushed down to carry up to William while leaving the empty ones for the girl to refill. The dogs were beside themselves, running back and forth in their confusion and barking fearfully. The Watsons were labouring steadily to douse the flaming missiles that landed on the roof. How much longer their energies and willpower would hold out was questionable. Olaf sprang from the canoe and tore up to Betty and took the buckets from her and rushed to the ladder. This allowed Josie a reprieve from the strenuous task while her mother took over. With Olaf on hand to help, it was not long before the shingles were sopping wet. Attention was next directed to clearing dried vegetation and debris away from the sides of the cabin. For several hours, the routine of drenching the roof and dousing hotspots around the building continued. The group's energy level and spirits were at a very, low ebb and they were fearful that they were losing the battle. Suddenly, as if by magic, the air cooled and the smoke filled atmosphere began to clear. The hungry inferno, following the fuel source, moved northward where it would come up against an expansive wet-land and eventually burn itself out.

Everyone halted what they were doing and looked at one another with disbelief and, when they realized that the danger had passed, their mouths stretched into wide, happy grins. They jumped up and down and danced around, howling and screaming with delight. The dogs entered into the game and leaped about, barking crazily, and chased each other around in circles. As if on command, all four dropped to the ground in utter exhaustion and lay there gasping and panting without speaking. William sat up and said that when he saw Olaf, it was like a miracle from heaven, he could not believe his eyes at first. They all relaxed on the dusty ground and listened to Olaf's tale about how he happened to be on hand. The Watsons fully believed that if their friend had not arrived when he did, the house would have been destroyed. One by one, led by Josie, fully clothed, they all waded out into the bay and sat down in the cool water until the heat and sweat of their bodies were dispelled. Dripping wet, they checked around the cabin area and put out the remaining hot-spots and William then cleared the roof of all smouldering chunks of wood. Inside, the cabin had to be aired and the white ash, that had settled in through the chimney, had to be cleaned away. The pungent smell and billowing puffs of lazy smoke would permeate the atmosphere for several days. How the fire started was any one's guess; by nature or human carelessness? Years will pass before nature could fully restore the forest to its original state.

Olaf stayed with the family for a week to help them restore the cabin and area around it. Using canoes, they freighted fire-wood from the region on the north side of the bay that had been bypassed. Fortunately, the shed that stored the traps, saws, axes and tools was spared due to its proximity to the water and being outside the perimeter of burning trees. The Watsons were thankful that things turned out as well as they had because they could have lost everything. William stated that he would have further to travel to maintain his trapping, but figured that within a year the animals will return to his usual area. At the end of the week, Olaf left the Watsons. He wished them well and said that he will look forward to seeing them the day before Jim was scheduled to airlift them to the Landing.

For miles along the west shoreline, he was overwhelmed by the desolation of the forest that once stood so majestically. The sandy areas of the shoreline were churned up by the feet of frantic animals fleeing the killer flames. A young bear's smouldering, scorched carcass lay in a heap on top of a rock outcropping and the sow, whining plaintively, was nudging it with its nose trying to get it to rise. She was oblivious to Olaf as the canoe glided past so close that he could have touched her with his paddle. Further along, he observed other pitiful scenes where animals had not escaped the fire's wrath. A doe and her fawn lay side by side about a hundred yards from the edge of safety, blackened to a crispy hardness; puffs of smoke rising from them like Indian smoke signals. From all appearances, it seemed the doe stayed with its exhausted, frightened baby while the fire raged across and killed them. A cow moose and her two young were standing waist deep in the water, their bulging, staring eyes depicted fear of the greatest depth. Olaf viewed the horrifying destruction of animals and forest with feelings of helplessness and nausea. Eventually he passed the bleak, burnt area redolent of charred and rotting flesh mixed with the pungent fumes from the smouldering vegetation. It was exhilarating to breathe in the clean, cool air. He paddled vigorously towards home feeling anxious and fearful about what he might find. Soon the cabin loomed into view and Olaf released a big sigh of relief, because it stood untouched. Inwardly, he thanked God for sparing his home and trapping area.

CHAPTER FIFTEEN
THE BIG DAY

Two weeks after the forest fire, the weather changed dramatically. Heavy, cumulous clouds were building to the north, darkening from dull grey to black. During the early hours, Olaf was wakened from a deep sleep by the rain crashing down on his roof as if a giant was practicing his percussion rudiments with large drum sticks. Joy was in his heart because the rain was much needed to dispel further dangers of the prolonged heat wave. For two days it poured in profusion and as soon as the drops hit the ground they were absorbed by the parched earth, like drops of ink on a blotter. The lake level rose and the Grass River flowed in spate, spilling mud and debris into the lake. When the storm passed, the sun shone brilliantly from an azure sky. The tumultuous rain had in effect cured the withered landscape; new life was restored to the land.

Time was passing quickly so Olaf spent the last week of July making the cabin presentable to receive Mary. He was glad that he had the forethought to have Ian order him a new suit, shirt, tie, socks and shoes, so now he did not have to worry about carrying an outfit from home. It was mid-week and he had just completed replenishing the supply of fire-wood when someone halloed from out on the lake, giving notice that he was approaching. At the sound of the voice, the dogs scurried to the beach and barked excitedly. Olaf shaded his eyes from the glare of the setting sun and peered out onto the lake where he saw a canoe approaching. As the craft glided up to the beach he recognized Gerald, the Chief, his wife, Ootah, and Totono, the Medicine Man. They each eased their cramped bodies from the canoe and limped up to the cabin. Hearty greetings were exchanged with handshakes and friendly backslapping. Gerald explained that they were on the way to the Trading Post to attend the wedding as representatives of the Fox Lake Band in honour of their brother and his bride. Olaf beamed with delight and expressed how proud he was to have them attend.

The setting sun was beginning to dip below the trees so Olaf invited them to stay the night and have supper with him. They gracefully accepted the invitation and pitched their tent on the flat ground in the grove of poplar trees. While they were setting up, Olaf went inside to prepare the meal. The group spent the evening talking about many things. Olaf learned a lot about the history and people of the Fox Lake Reserve. The visitors left early the next day.

Olaf's social life was at an all-time high because, two days later, the Watsons appeared on the scene. There was a lot of gleeful excitement during the final preparations for the air journey to the Post the following day.

Jim arrived the next morning as scheduled and the weather could not have been more co-operative. It was balmy and wisps of flimsy clouds floated lazily across the blue sky. After a light snack, the dogs and all the personal belongings were loaded and the party were lifted into the air at high-noon. Jodie was overcome with excitement, as this was her first ride in a plane. She marvelled at the sight of everything below as they whisked their way over the lake and trees. In a relatively short time, Jim was banking the craft for its approach to the landing. The people on the shore watched the plane make its descent and lightly touch down on the glass like surface. Eager hands were ready to moor the plane, greet the passengers and aid in unloading the gear. The assemblage, heading up to the Post with Angus in the forefront, resembled the scene from the Pied Piper of Hamlin where the children were being lured to an unknown destiny.

The remaining part of the day was spent in completing last minute preparations and a brief rehearsal for the wedding. Mary and Betty spent a great deal of time together discussing women's things, each an elixir for the other, especially for Betty because she had lacked adult, female companionship for several years, except when she visited the post once a year. Emma had prepared a sumptuous evening meal that was served on the lawn, buffet style. Mary's family, feeling very much at home, mingled with the people and Olaf made a special point of introducing Gerald, Ootah and Totono to Mary and her family.

CHAPTER SIXTEEN
THE WEDDING DAY

It poured during the night but, by early morning, the rain had tapered off to a fine drizzle which ceased before the sun was barely in the sky. The day was made fresh and cool by a gentle breeze that drifted off the lake.

The ceremony was scheduled for two thirty so the morning was hectic with preparations in all quarters. Persons were seeing to the needs of the nervous bride-to-be and the equally nervous groom. Emma, with her army of assistants, was very busy putting the final touches to the food preparation and Angus had placed himself in charge of seeing to the liquid refreshments, alcoholic and non-alcoholic. At the appointed time for attendance at the church, the entire hive of industry seemed to stop as if a referee had blown his whistle and the people of the village were summoned to the church by the pealing of the ancient, iron bell. The building was filled to capacity and those who weren't early enough to get seats behind those reserved for the family and friends, stood packed, shoulder to shoulder, like sardines in a can. The groom and the best man were standing rigidly before the gowned priest like two misbehaved boys called up on the carpet before the principal. While awaiting the appearance of the bride, there were the usual sounds of restless, shuffling feet, periodic, subdued coughing and throat clearing, sniffing, children fidgeting and the monotonous buzzing of flies against the window panes. Heads turned towards the door at the sound of feet scuffling up the path and, as if by magic, the bride and her father, preceded by Josie, the flower girl, loomed in the opening. At that moment the organist pounded out the wedding march on the old, out-of-tune organ. Mary looked like a princess in her elegant dress of fine, white linen and the lacy veil covering her face. A respectful hush settled throughout the church as the pair stood before the priest. Olaf, looking out of place in a suit, felt himself tremble nervously from head to toe during the ceremony. When Father Beleau proclaimed them to be man and wife, the entire congregation broke out with laughter and clapping and as the newly weds left the church they were showered with dried flower petals. A horse drawn wagon whisked them away from the crowd to the Factor's house where they had some time to themselves before the guests arrived.

By four o'clock the guests, comprised of the entire village, had gradually assembled on the front lawn and feasted on the variety of delectable foods laid out on long, wooden tables and socialized throughout the afternoon.

The wedding gifts were placed on a plank table and, as the festivities went on, the pile grew and grew to resemble a small hill. An accordion and fiddle materialized from out of the blue and in no time the toe tapping renditions had people dancing. The sun was beginning its downward dip when the partiers were summoned to gather around in front of the gift table. Mary and Olaf unwrapped and acknowledged each gift with their heart felt thanks. The gifts were a variety of household goods, food, decorative items, cooking utensils and the Fox Lake Tribe gave moose-hide slippers, moccasins, and jackets decorated with dyed porcupine quills.

At eleven o'clock the newly weds excused themselves from their guests and retired to the honey-moon suite that Emma had especially prepared for them in the main house. At mid-night, Angus called a halt to the festivities and thanked all for attending and suggested that if they wanted to see the newly-weds off in the morning, they should be at the landing by ten o'clock. Those that had remained to the last, quietly dispersed like autumn leaves before a gentle breeze. The last to leave the scene were the dogs who eagerly scavenged for food scraps all around and under the tables.

The next morning, the newly weds gathered with their friends and Mary's family at a wedding breakfast. There was much joy and playful bantering back and forth at their expense. Eventually the time arrived when they had to depart. Mary, with Olaf, spent a few private moments with her family before boarding the plane.

A large group of well-wishers gathered at the beach to see the newly weds and the Watsons off. Jim made a low pass over the village and the passengers had an excellent view of the crowd standing on the shore.

In no time at all, the aircraft landed at the cabin. Everyone managed to avoid getting wet when they alit, except the dogs, who immediately leapt into the water and paddled about like children in a wading pool.

As Mary stood and gazed at her new home for the very first time, tears of emotional happiness trickled down her cheeks. It was more than what she had imagined from the description Olaf gave of it. This log building was now her home and it was the place where she will be beginning a new life with her husband, the man she loved. Feelings of happiness and contentment flooded into her heart. She passionately hugged and kissed Olaf and then sprinted to the cabin.

The rest stayed behind as Olaf carried her over the threshold; both giggling and kissing as they entered their home. After an interval of several long minutes, the joyous couple appeared and beckoned to their friends to come in.

Mary invited the group stay for something to eat before leaving. Jim declined as he had to get back to base and do a short run before nightfall. The Watsons remained long enough to have a meal and a visit before they departed.

CHAPTER SEVENTEEN
A TRAPPER'S WIFE

Mary took up the role of a trapper's wife with ease. Using the skills taught by her mother, she had transformed the rustic cabin into a veritable, cosy abode. She was dexterous in every way. Olaf was overjoyed that she was able to adjust to this way of life. Her intelligence, personality, vitality and spirit blended together to prepare her for what lay ahead in becoming a trapper's wife.

Olaf introduced Mary to the ways of trapping. They travelled to his line camps and worked to ready them for the season ahead. Fishing and hunting were parts of the trapper's life that she, at first, was hesitant to be party to but, under her husband's patient instruction, she became very adept in these as well as setting traps, skinning and preparing hides. Outdoor cooking methods were also added to her list of skills. It was not long before she became proficient as the front paddle handler in the canoe. Weighted down with a back-pack, she moved effortlessly along the trails and kept up with Olaf all the way. He taught her how to bait and set the various types of traps. She aptly accepted this way of life, which was a boon to him. His work-load had reduced and the returns were greatly increased. In time, she qualified as a bona fide trapper's wife.

In mid October Mary had experienced a near, fatal event. The trees were adorned in fall colours and the day was comfortably warm. Olaf suggested that they make a hunt up the Grass River for meat. She had never hunted big game before so this would be a new adventure. They each carried a rifle and a back pack containing their lunch, change of socks and an extra sweater. They hiked northward along the river and, after an hour, turned west into a meadows dotted with several large, marshy ponds. Olaf whispered that in this area, they will likely see moose because they frequented it to feed on the lush grasses that grew around the ponds. They followed a well used game trail that skirted the edge of the first pond. It then edged its way along a narrow canal that joined up to the second pond which was hidden from view by a stand of birch and jack-pines. At the end of the wood lot, they saw three fat, cow moose feeding in the shallows. Olaf signalled for Mary to remain at this spot with the dogs while he checked the area for a bull that might be around as this was the rut. He cautioned her to stay still and not to make a noise. After what seemed an eternity to her, Mary threw caution to the wind and cautiously stepped through the trees and out onto the pond's shore to gain a better view of what Olaf was doing. The dogs were quiet but they appeared to be agitated and she wondered why. Carelessly she took a long stride forward and stepped on a dead branch that sounded like the snap of a bull whip when it broke. Off to her right, outside the periphery of her vision, a massive bull moose was standing, watching over his cows. When the branch snapped, the beast pivoted on the spot and faced Mary. He glared at her through blood shot eyes, snorted angrily, pawed the ground and, with unbelievable speed, charged towards the interloper who dared to enter his domain. The loud grunts and bellowing alerted Olaf to the danger and he sprinted like a marathon runner to the scene. Mary stood transfixed to the spot, terror grasping her by the throat so she couldn't scream. A hundred yards from her the moose was briefly distracted by Thor and Kyla who rushed dangerously close in front of it and barked menacingly. The bull easily chased the dogs by threatening them with his enormous rack and then turned his attention to his target. Olaf appeared on the scene, sized up the situation, got down on one knee, took aim and fired. The high calibre bullet smashed into the bull's right shoulder causing him to loose balance, tumble and skid forward on its side. It ended up about ten yards from her. Although stunned and wounded, the outraged bull was determined to reach his foe. In a blind fury and hateful rage, he pushed with his hind legs and pulled with his good front leg and inched his way towards her. Olaf stepped forward and put the animal out of its misery with a well placed bullet to the head. He reached out to Mary and gently led her away from the scene. They sat down and tightly held one another. Both were trembling, Mary from fright and shock, Olaf from relief and the fear of what it may have been had he been further away and didn't arrive in time.

They talked about the event over their lunch. Mary stated that had she not been so stupid and did as she was told this probably would not have happened but she was not deterred from hunting in the future. They decided not to take any of the moose for meat as it was very thin and would not be good eating. The bulls do not eat prior to and during the rut because they have only one thing on their minds, cow moose. Instead, they settled for a fat cow.

In the evening, they sat on the porch, and watched the sun slip out of sight and the silvery, harvest moon inch its way over the tree tops. They did not speak, but sat in contented silence. When it became too cool to stay out, they went inside and closed the door on the day's events.

CHAPTER EIGHTEEN
PRINCESS RAVEN HAIR

During the latter part of October, a light, smoky haze hung like a lacy curtain over the land. The warm Indian Summer Days were an idyllic prelude to winter. The Svensons were very busy stocking the larder, laying in a generous supply of wood and readying the traps. The line-camps had been seen to during the summer and now were ready for the season. When all the pre-winter chores had been completed and favourable weather had persisted for several weeks, Olaf suggested that they take advantage of the time left and visit the Fox Lake Reserve and the Watsons. If all goes well they should be back within two weeks and be at home when Jim arrives from the south with their supplies.

The sun was barely up when they pulled away from the shore and paddled effortlessly toward Herblet Lake. The last of the ghostly, morning mist had been wafted into thin air by the soft, warm breezes that skimmed along the lake's surface. Large flocks of migrating geese floated like an armada on the still waters in the quiet bays along with noisy ducks. Several cow moose and their young were spotted feeding in the shallows of the inlets. As they passed through the narrows leading into Herblet Lake they saw, through the crystal clear water, large lake trout lazily floating like submerged logs as if waiting to be hand-plucked out of the water. The reflected sunlight glistened like polished jewels bobbing on the wavelets. All four travellers were at peace with the world, mesmerized by the wonders of nature.

It was mid-morning when they nudged the canoe onto the beach where the tall, solitary pine stood like a sentinel on guard at the entrance of the trail to Fox Lake. After a hasty mug-up, they stored the canoe and then, with their back-packs securely in place, took to the trail. The air was hot and their perspiration attracted the hated mosquitoes that attacked ferociously like miniature spit-fires. They made several stops to rest and dry their sweaty faces and arms: the dogs flopped down with their pink tongues lolling out the side of their gaping, panting mouths. Eventually they reached the opening that looked down upon the settlement and there they paused to view the scene before them. It was a hive of industry below. Racks of split trout and white-fish, perched over fires of smouldering green logs, were being smoked and thin strips of moose meat were hung out to cure in the hot sun in preparation for making pemmican, dried meat slices finely pounded, rolled in rendered fat, mixed with berries and then stored in skin pouches for future consumption. Several native men were out in the bay hauling in nets filled with struggling fish. Four women were skinning a moose and a deer that were hanging head down from strong tree limbs and several others were scaling and gutting fish. Older children could be seen gathering wood for the curing fires while the younger children romped about and played games.

As they strolled down the hill to the settlement, the tethered dogs rose in unison and greeted them with a combination of barks, yips and baying. All in the village stopped and peered, squinting against the sun, in wonderment at the two people and dogs entering their territory. The first to give recognition was Gerald, the chief, who came briskly towards them, his face beaming expansively. He vigorously pumped their hands and loudly proclaimed how happy he was to have them visit the reserve. Like moths attracted to a light, the people gathered about with expressions of delight and gleeful chuckles. A couple of young lads were dispatched to inform Anyiato that Gentle Spirit and his woman will be coming to see her. En masse they headed towards Anyiato's cabin, looking not unlike a mob with a purpose. When they arrived, she was standing in the doorway supporting her frail body with a stout cane. Tears flowed heavily down her brown cheeks and fell to the floor like raindrops and her toothless gums showed as she laughed and gibbered in Cree. She embraced Mary and hauled her into the cabin and Olaf followed. Gerald turned to the crowd and told them to return to their jobs and work hard as tomorrow will be a day of celebration in honour of their guests.

The next day's events ended with a gathering in the community hall where feasting, dancing and games of competition took place. The chief, Totono and several elders made speeches and presented the guests, who sat next to Anyiato at the head table, with gifts. During a lull in the festivities, Totono arose, waved his decorated wand and called for silence. The chief stood and announced that Gentle Spirit had been ceremoniously welcomed into the tribe, so must his woman be likewise welcomed. The chief and elders made speeches that proclaimed their pleasure to have Mary as an honorary member of the tribe. The Medicine Man then conducted the ceremonial ritual and proclaimed that Mary, in keeping with her shiny black hair, is named Princess Raven Hair.

Early the next day, Princess Raven Hair and Gentle Spirit departed from the village, their backpacks heavy with many gifts. The entire populace was present to see them off. They hugged Anyiato, suspecting in their minds that she will have passed away before they next returned. Her wizened, frail body trembled, even though she tried to keep a stiff upper lip, and her eyes welled over copiously when Olaf held her in his arms and when Mary embraced her. Anyiato mumbled in Cree that Mary was her adopted daughter and prayed to the spirits to look upon them favourably and bless them with many happy, healthy papooses. With a last look back and a final wave, the couple left their friends.

The morning air was cool and they made good progress along the trail towards Herblet Lake. Crispy leaves crackled under their feet and the gentle, autumn breeze caressed their tanned faces. At the lake, during the mug-up with moose jerky and bannock, they discussed the events of the past days and each expressed their views and sentiments. Mary stated that this experience will forever be a highlight in her life.

It was an easy paddle across the mirror like surface and very little was said, for each was engrossed in their personal thoughts and allowed themselves the luxury of enjoying the tranquillity of the glorious, autumn day. Thus the miles slid by effortlessly and by noon they arrived at the Watson's. There was great delight all around when the humans and animals greeted each other. The two days of visiting passed quickly and it seemed as if there was not enough time to make the most of the get-together. It was established that the Watsons would come to the Svensons early in November, ahead of the freeze-up, when Betty, Josie and Mary will stay with all the dogs while the men make a trip to the trading post for supplies.

CHAPTER NINETEEN
THE TRIP TO THE POST

On the second day of November, in the late afternoon, the Watsons arrived drenched and chilled to the bone due to the icy drizzle that had worked its way down from the arctic regions. The cosy warm cabin and hot food erased all memory of the discomfort they had experienced. The men agreed that the round trip to the post had to be expeditious because winter conditions can strike quickly without any warning. Plans were made for an early start. Several hours quickly passed by over hot cups of coffee and much conversing. Many stifled yawns indicated that all were ready to hit the sack so, with mumbled good nights, they dispersed to their beds.

At the break of day under a heavy sky, Olaf and William left for the trading post, each paddling his own canoe. The wives and Josie stood on the shore waving goodbye. The unhappy dogs, perplexed as to why they were not going, ran along the shore barking their disappointment and went back only after much calling by the women and stern reprimands to go back from the men.

It was an unpleasant day. A strong, frigid breeze flung an icy spray from the choppy waters onto the paddlers. After several hours of strenuous paddling, Pierre Deboise's forlorn cabin loomed into view as they rounded the point of the bay. They hastily beached their crafts and ran to the cabin to prepare a fire for their lunch break. Olaf had difficulty in getting the kindling to ignite because he kept dropping the matches due to his fingers being stiff and clumsy because of the freezing temperature. Eventually he had a huge bon-fire going, around which they huddled to capture the comforting, radiated heat. The cold moose meat sandwiches, lightly toasted on the embers, were greatly enjoyed, followed by quaffs of hot tea. Feeling greatly revived, the men continued the journey. An hour before they reached the post's landing, they were assaulted by a shower of icy snow which blew directly at them obscuring their vision. Ice was building up on the gunwales, paddles and their clothing. Progress was slow and the paddling tedious because of the excessive weight from the ice. The last hour of travel was the most difficult because they had to strain their muscles to the extreme to keep the canoes on a forward course. Suddenly, through a brief break in the snow-storm they sighted the beach. Every muscle ached as they made the final push to get to the landing through a carpet of slush that lay on the lake's surface. There was no welcoming committee at the beach because everyone was cosily secluded in their homes and did not expect any die hard fools to be out in this foul weather.

They pulled their crafts well up onto the beach and turned them over and tied them to the anchor pegs. As it was past closing time, the men hurried up to the factor's house and knocked loudly on the heavy pine door. A moment passed before Ian flung open the door and instantly his face registered disbelief and at the same time extreme pleasure when he saw his unexpected visitors. Ushering them into the warm living room, he led the two men to the huge, blazing fireplace and bade them to strip off their cold, damp outer wear. Emma entered the room and with squeals of delight she rushed to Olaf and William and gave each a big hug. After a period of excited visitation and several rounds of hot rum toddy the group sat down to a well deserved, hot supper. It was opportune that Emma had made a pot of stew and baked fresh bread that afternoon.

The following day, Olaf and William selected and assembled their purchases and squared off their accounts with Ian. After supper a cosy evening was spent in front of the fire place. Being that they planned to leave early in the morning, the travellers took to their beds before midnight.

They pulled away from the landing very early in a dense, chilling mist that shrouded the lake and reduced the visibility considerably. Moisture clung to everything the mist touched and added to their discomfort until the sun burned off some of the fog by mid-morning. The steady breeze from the north did not allow the warmth from the blazing sun to be of benefit. The canoes were loaded to such an extent that the gunwales were just inches above the water, thus they crowded the shoreline and travelled in the shallow regions in case the wind increased in intensity and caused waves to splash over into the canoes. Rather than go to the effort of beaching for their lunch break, they remained in the canoes and munched on the sandwiches and raisin biscuits. Paddling was laboriously slow and uncomfortable, perspiration soaked their bodies and, when they stopped working the paddles, the icy breeze chilled them through. The pressing journey, though tedious, was uneventful except when a grunting, enraged bull moose, in rut, plunged part way through the shallows along the shore and snorted a challenge to them. It was late in the afternoon when they spotted the cabin with its glowing, yellow windows and saw the smoke lazily float away into the dusk. As they got nearer, the dogs appeared on the shore and noisily welcomed them home. The women appeared on the embankment and frantically waved and hollered as the men approached the beach. The joyous homecoming made the tedious journey seem like nothing more than a mere picnic.

Olaf offered William the loan of his canoe to transport his family comfortably and tow his home without being dangerously crowded in the one canoe. He said that he and Mary would hike over before freeze-up to visit and pick it up then. It was not until that visit, a week later, did they learn about the Watson's near perilous journey home.

Fortunately, William had the foresight to have everyone don their waterproof oil slickers before setting out. About an hour into their trip an easterly wind started to blow which, at first, did not concern them. Soon its force increased considerably, causing very choppy conditions and impeding the steering of the canoes. Icy spray blew into their faces and water slopped over into the canoe. Betty frantically bailed and it took all of William's efforts to keep the crafts on course. The dogs and Josie were huddled on the bottom of the boat to lessen the force of the storm lashing at their bodies. To make matters worse, the gusting winds thrust heavy sprays of freezing rain at them and further built the on-rushing waves higher than the gunnels of the canoes. The two crafts bobbed up and down like corks and each time the bows came down they smacked the water heavily with resounding slaps that shook them from front to end. The situation was now becoming very dangerous because the rain increased in intensity and obliterated their vision. William strained every muscle to keep them moving forward. At this desperate moment, he made a crucial decision to steer an oblique course towards the shore because had he turned directly into the shore the tumbling waves would overflow into the back end of the canoe and cause them to flounder and possibly sink. The canoe behind was at the mercy of the wind and waves. It tossed and bucked like an angry bronco and tugged at the line, straining it to the breaking point. Just before they reached the safety of the beach, the tow line snapped and the cargo canoe went adrift on a course dictated by the pounding waves. William rapidly plunged the paddle in and out of the water to force the craft well up onto the sand. Leaving Betty and Josie to pull it up high and away from the grip of the lashing water, he stepped into the water at the expense of getting a little water into his rubber boots, grabbed the tow line and hauled the canoe back to the shore where he and Betty, with all their strength, heaved it onto land out of reach of the angry waves that pummelled the shore with a vengeance. They hauled the empty canoe onto the grassy verge, turned it over with its bottom against the wind and rain, crawled under it and huddled together with Josie in the middle and the dogs on either side.

The storm raged for several hours before it abated and, about two hours before sunset, the wind and rain abruptly stopped, leaving the lake reasonably calm except for small wavelets playing across the surface. They took advantage of the moment and scrambled from beneath the canoe. William secured the cargo canoe with a shorter line and they headed for home, extremely chilled but, thanks to the slickers, only slightly damp. The rest of the journey was uneventful and they arrived home in the fading light. Betty saw to Josie and got the stove going while William unloaded the cargo which suffered some wetness but thankfully not enough to cause any spoilage. The worst that the family experienced from the ordeal was some minor coughing and sniffles which, left them within the week.

CHAPTER TWENTY
MARY'S ORDEAL

November and December yielded the Svensons an abundant harvest of pelts. Mary proved to be a very efficient asset to the partnership. She learned the art of trapping so well that Olaf assigned her an area for which she was entirely responsible. This division allowed them to harvest more skins in a shorter time frame than when Olaf ran the whole show himself. Thus, by mid December, they had a consignment of prime furs ready to ship when Jim was due to drop off the winter supplies before Christmas.

On a very chilly morning, Mary peered through a partially frosted window pane and saw that the lake was covered over with a skin of ice that stretched outwardly from the shore. Olaf predicted that if the cold weather held, the entire lake will be iced over and safe enough for travel within a week

One afternoon, Mary and Olaf had just returned from a successful moose hunt. From the north, they saw heavy, dark, ominous, cumulous clouds rushing towards them like a herd of stampeding cattle. By the time they had finished unloading the gear and the meat, swirls of snowflakes began to gently descend like tossed confetti. At bed time, a whiteout blizzard was furiously buffeting the landscape. It blew all of the next day and, sometime during the night, it petered out, leaving in its wake a landscape drowned in an ocean of pure whiteness.

Olaf was pleased with the snow as it would make their trapping rounds easier to traverse. The day after the storm, they made an afternoon's journey, using the dogs and sled, to retrieve the rest of the moose meat that had been left hanging high above the ground. The weather remained cold and unsettled for several days, forcing them to stay in-doors.

It was during these periods of such inclement weather that time was devoted to doing things around the cabin. Mary gave her attention and efforts to tidying up the cabin, doing laundry, cooking, baking and knitting. The cabin was relatively easy to keep in order, because she swept, dusted and arranged shelves and cupboards regularly. The laundry in itself was a tedious and lengthy chore as it required much physical effort for which she commandeered Olaf's strength for assistance. Her greatest pleasures were cooking and baking. Olaf enjoyed fresh baked breads, cookies, pies, stews, roasts, soups and the old stand-by, baked beans with molasses and chunks of fatty, moose meat. She prepared frozen meals for quick preparation when coming home after being on the trail and, as well, food portions for the trail and line camps. Olaf was busy splitting wood and kindling, hauling water, catching fish, cleaning and stretching hides, as well as doing a host of other jobs required to keep the cabin comfortable and functional. Winter evenings at home were relaxing. Mary would sit by the stove in her home-made rocking chair, knitting and Olaf would be in his rocking chair on the other side, puffing on his pipe while reading and the dogs would sleep, stretched flat-out in front. When the transmission of radio waves came in clear of static and crackling, they would listen to the wireless.

Two days after they had returned from the trap lines, Jim flew in with the goods ordered from Winnipeg. The day was sunny and very crispy, at minus twenty. He visited for two hours and enjoyed the warmth of the cabin and the generous hospitality. The news from the south was that there was an influenza epidemic prevalent in the cities and towns from which many elderly and young had died, an influx of immigrants into Manitoba, Saskatchewan and Alberta were taking up land for farming, the price of fur was holding steady and the newspapers are carrying stories of discontentment of the labour force over wages and working conditions.

Jim spun the motor and let it idle while he and Olaf loaded the bundles of fur. Soon after, he taxied the craft out to the middle of the lake and took off, with a roar, into the prevailing wind and, once airborne, he circled around and flew low, tilted the wings up and down and then swooped away into the blue, leaving two arm-waving figures standing in front of the cabin.

On their previous visit to the Watsons, it was arranged that Mary and Olaf would come and spend Christmas with them. On the morning of December 24, the sun barely risen, the Svensons, using the hard snow-packed lake as their highway, headed out. The sky was cloudless and the brilliant sun blazed like a lantern, offering light but no warmth. One knew that the temperature was far below zero from the squeal the runners made on the hard-packed snow, the loud, grinding crunch Olaf's moccasins made as he ran behind, the clouds of frozen mist coming from their mouths, the tingling iciness of the frigid air moving against their skin and Mary, though well blanketed in the sled, had to periodically slap her moose-mitt covered hands together and wiggle her toes to keep the blood circulating.

The journey was uneventful until a pack of six bush wolves, howling in full bay, emerged suddenly from the forest and loped along the shore-ice about two hundred yards abreast of the Svensons. They did not initially seem to pose any danger but, after a while, the leader began to narrow the gap making Olaf somewhat uncomfortable. The dogs were agitated and nervous and Mary voiced some worrying concerns. It was Olaf's guess that they were interested in Kyla and Thor for a snack. The situation was beginning to take a sinister turn due to the boldness of the pack so Olaf stopped the team, retrieved the rifle from the sled and fired several warning shots in front of them. This tactic delayed the wolves momentarily after which they renewed their harassment more vigorously. Suddenly, they veered in front of the them in order to cut them off. Olaf took the next desperate action. He killed the leader. This action immediately disoriented the pack and caused them to drop back and give up the chase. Olaf hurriedly moved on and when he looked back, he saw the pack tearing at the carcass of their leader, devouring it in great gulps - hunger being a stronger need than loyalty to a fallen comrade.

At high noon Olaf steered the team towards the shore and stopped in amongst a growth of thickets which gave them some protection from the icy breeze. A blazing fire provided them with physical and psychological warmth. The blackened tea-pail was packed with snow and hung over the fire. When it came to the boil, Olaf placed it at the edge of the fire and threw in some tea leaves, sugar and powdered milk. The brew and toasted sandwiches gave them renewed energy to continue their journey.

It was mid afternoon when, in the distance, they spotted Watson's cosy cabin, snuggled in the snow covered landscape against a backdrop of fire charred trees. Olaf stopped and fired off a shot to announce their arrival and, by the time they reached the cabin, the Watsons and the dogs came spilling out through the cabin door, excited and eager as any welcoming committee could ever be. The Svensons and Watsons enjoyed Christmas and welcomed in the New Year. On Mary's invitation, Betty promised that they will come to visit in early May, after the ice went out. On the morning of January 2, 1922, Mary and Olaf took their leave of their hosts. The temperature was well below zero and a brilliant, rising sun was edging its way into a clear blue sky. Travel conditions were excellent. They made good time on the return journey and as they passed the place where the wolves had intimidated them, they saw a large circle of bloodied snow with chunks of fur and the odd pieces of bone lying about. They arrived home in the late afternoon with Jack Frost nipping at their heels.

Two days later, Mary and Olaf journeyed to their trap lines. Olaf broke trail for the dogs while Mary followed behind. They arrived at Camp Number One when the sun was at its zenith. After a quick mug-up, they set the traps around the frozen swamp. Early, the next morning they retrieved the trapped animals and reset the traps. The same procedure was repeated at Camp Number Two. The frozen carcasses were securely stored in the line shacks to be picked up on their way back. They looked forward to the stay at Dead Bear Camp as it was larger and more comfortable. They arrived as the day was giving way to dusk and the temperature plunged considerably, so no time was available for setting traps. Olaf soon had the metal camp-stove humming with the burning tinder and dry logs and laid out the sleeping bags on a mattress of fresh, spruce boughs. Mary placed slabs of frozen stew in the sizzling frying pan, warmed up some frozen bannock and brewed a strong pot of tea. After consuming the gourmet, wilderness meal, the camp was prepared for the night. Olaf toted in several large logs to place in the stove and set the damper so they would burn slowly during the night to provide a comfortable temperature that would stave off the frost. Mary set aside bannock and honey on the floor close to the stove to keep warm and ready for breakfast. The tea pail was replenished with snow and placed at the back of the stove to melt and heat during the night. The combination of a satisfying meal, the cosiness of the shack and the tiredness from a day's travel in the cold brought down the heavy veil of sleep over them. As they slept they were oblivious to the silence of the forest being interrupted by the rifle-shot sounds of trees splitting due to the rigours of the very low temperatures and the distant chorus of a wolf pack in full chase of some doomed quarry.

The day's routine was that Mary, with Kyla, would work the shallow end of the lake for the smaller animals such as weasel, marten and rats and Olaf, with Thor, would travel further into the forest to set traps for fox, bobcat and wolf. By mid afternoon they were to be back at the camp to compare notes on the work completed. When the day began, the sky was a solid, dirty grey and the sun struggled to shine through. As the morning progressed, a northerly wind blew in and the clouds became ominously dark. Olaf was on his way back to the line camp as gentle flakes began to descend over the landscape. He didn't give it much thought because he knew that he would be back with Mary within the hour. Within a short time, the weather became more unsettled and the snow fell with greater intensity, making good vision next to impossible. Thor was ahead, sniffing out the way, keeping Olaf on track.

As they approached the camp, Kyla came bounding through the drifts to greet them. Olaf hollered as he yanked opened the door and to his dismay there was no sign of Mary. Outside, around the camp, there were no fresh tracks to indicate that she had been there since morning. His stomach felt heavy and knotted up and fear gripped at his heart, causing him to panic. Something must have happened to her and either she sent Kyla back or the animal came back on her own. Sensing something amiss, he quickly hitched Thor to the sled and commanded Kyla to go get Mary. The dog immediately ran off in the direction from whence she came. It was tough going as the snow was continuing its descent in full force and the wind was blowing snow at the travellers with a blizzard force. Kyla, after what seemed like hours, came to an open area at the end of the frozen swamp. There was no sign of Mary but Kyla with an excited whimper ran about sniffing every inch of the place. Suddenly with a high pitched yelp she ran towards what seemed to be a long, snow covered mound and began scratching away the snow. Olaf knew that this was Mary and he hurriedly ploughed his way through the deep snow to her side. Using his hands as scoops, he frantically pulled the deep snow away from her body. Mary did not respond to his shaking and calling her name; she appeared to be in a trance.

He established that she had a weak pulse which spurred him on to get her back to camp as she was suffering from hypothermia. In no time he had her loaded onto the sled and placed his parka over her. Kyla was hitched up with Thor and the team headed out. The group plodded through the ever deepening snow and pushed against the pounding wind and lashing snow that seemed determined to prevent them from reaching the camp. Normally they would have been home within a half hour, but an hour or more passed before they drew up to the door. Exhausted as he was, Olaf's inner strength surfaced to allow him to get Mary unloaded into the shack and lay her down on the spruce-bough mattress. He stuffed the stove with dry, feathered kindling and split logs and with trembling fingers got a fire blazing. Next, he removed her outer clothing and moccasins and vigorously rubbed her feet, and arms which, along with the heat, brought renewed colour to her face and her skin began to feel warm. Mary's pulse gradually increased and soon she stirred from her stupor. Olaf, supported her in a sitting position and gently forced hot tea through her cracked lips; she swallowed in small gulps. He was relieved to see her return to normal and, while she slept, he intently watched over her like a mother hen. As he placed her into the sleeping bag, Olaf was alarmed to see that her left knee was swollen and there was some bruising over the right ribs. These, he knew were the tell-tale marks of an accident.

Olaf was just finishing his third cup of tea when he heard Mary whimper and noticed her face grimace in pain. She opened her heavy lidded eyes with difficulty and moved her head about and looked around with a puzzled expression. Her eyes eventually focussed on Olaf and she asked in a husky whisper about what happened. He explained the events that led him to her and how he brought her back but other than that, he did not know what had happened. Her mind was blank and she could not at this time impart as to what did occur. After Mary had some food and hot liquid, he packed snow around the swelling to alleviate the pain and pressure and bound her tender ribs with strips of cloth torn from his cotton shirt. Surprisingly, she had a reasonable night and slept well. It was still snowing when they awoke, but the storm had down-scaled considerably from a blizzard.

Olaf coaxed the smouldering fire into lively flames. For breakfast they snacked on warmed bannock and fried beans washed down with coffee. The meal and cosy warmth brought Mary around to feeling better and she was able to sit up, propped against the wall, with the sleeping bag wrapped tightly around her. Through Olaf's coaxing questions, Mary pieced the story together as to what had happened.

She and Kyla arrived at the trapping area about mid-morning and made good progress in setting the traps. They had a light lunch before tackling the rugged north shore. Rather than go the long way around on the less dangerous trail, she opted to cross over the windfalls that interlaced the ground with a hazardous tumble of twisted and broken trees in order to save time in getting to the opposite side. She gingerly stepped her way through and over the dead trees and before she could reach the level ground, several yards away, she had to climb over a large, dead tree. She managed to crawl up onto its slippery surface and stood up to better view the rest of the route. While she was doing this, Kyla ran underneath the trees from where she flushed out a very large, angry weasel-like creature that snarled and hissed, baring its white, sharp teeth as its lips curled back into wrinkled furrows, making it appear extremely vicious. Mary, unexpectedly startled, lost her footing and fell from the tree, twisted her knee and slammed her body against the iron hard trunk. Because this all happened so quickly, she did not get a good look at the animal which disappeared as quickly as it had appeared. Kyla nervously crept to her side, whimpering and trembling, and looked around apprehensively. After overcoming the shock of the fall, Mary painfully crawled to the shore and propped herself against the tree where Olaf found her.

Realizing her precarious situation, she kept ordering Kyla to go home, knowing that Olaf would come looking when the dog showed up alone, but the distraught animal was reluctant to go and seemed puzzled as to what was expected. Mary carefully shuffled about to make herself comfortable against the insidious cold and excruciating pain. She remembered that her mind was becoming disoriented and she was mumbling complaints about the cold and pain before she slipped into a state of unconsciousness. It was after this that Kyla must have instinctively sensed that she had to get home to Olaf. The falling snow blanketed Mary and provided her with some insulation against the falling temperature. Olaf listened intently and when she related the part about the vicious animal, his entire body seemed to freeze momentarily and then vehemently blurted out that another Carcajou has moved into his area.

They stayed for two more nights before starting out for home. The storm left the area like the proverbial lamb and warmer weather pervaded for the next several days. With Mary comfortably loaded onto the sled, they headed for the cabin in the first light. Olaf planned to come back for the animal pelts in a few days time. The swelling of Mary's knee had gone down a little and she was feeling more at ease in moving it slightly up and down, but still, was unable to stand or walk without some support. Olaf made a set of crude crutches from sturdy, forked tree branches which allowed her to move about the cabin.

Three days after returning home, Olaf left to make the rounds of the line camps to retrieve the furs and frozen carcasses. He left Kyla with Mary and the cabin well stocked with wood and water. Olaf returned on the third day and was pleasantly surprised to see that Chief Gerald and his wife were visiting with Mary. They were on their way back to Fox Lake from a trip to the Hudson's Bay post. They had arrived several hours before Olaf and happily accepted the invitation to stay the night.

Olaf related the incident of Mary's accident and how Carcajou's sudden appearance led to her injuries. He asked Gerald if he knew of a way to rid his area of the hated wolverine. Gerald explained how the Indians use the Cubby Set trap as a sure method of taking the animal. The Cubby is placed against a sturdy tree using small poles to make the sides and roof and a square entrance of about twelve to fourteen inches. The bait is then placed at the back of the Cubby just above the trap that was hidden under a pile of rotted pine needles or snow. The trap must be tied to a heavy log or drag to prevent the animal from tearing up the Cubby as it would if the trap was secured to a chain attached to the tree. This information elated Olaf as he now felt less threatened with the presence of the stink weasel.

Gerald and Ootah took their leave early the next day. Gerald extended an invitation to his hosts to visit Fox Lake when they could. He mentioned that Anyioto was not well and would be more than pleased to see them.

CHAPTER TWENTY ONE

BAD TIMES

Mary's knee and ribs were not sufficiently healed to allow her to accompany Olaf on the trap lines. Thus, he had to make more trips to accomplish what he and Mary could have done in less time together. He didn't despair over the situation, but went ahead resolutely, keeping in mind that she would be waiting for his return and welcome him with all the niceties afforded a husband after a trying time on the job. This gave him greater impetus to get around the area so that he would not be away too long. The time without Mary on the line seemed to go by quickly knowing that she will soon be back on the run in several weeks, but, before she did, Olaf had in mind to deal with Carcajou.

There were signs of the wolverine's presence throughout his trapping space. On several occasions the devil skunk had sullied some of his catches and had succeeded in breaking into Camp One and, as if on a personal vendetta, left it in such an unliveable mess. Olaf declared all-out war on this creature as he had its predecessor. He recalled the instructions that Gerald had given him about making a Cubby Set Trap so he made that a first priority on this trip. He constructed the trap in the Camp Two region where most of Carcajou's evil work had been done. The first visit to the Cubby was disappointing because a huge raven, a trash animal, one that is of no use to the trapper, was dead in the trap. He reset the trap with new bait, but went one step further, he placed two leg traps side-by-side.

Olaf returned to the trap late in the afternoon the next day. The area around the tree looked like a war zone. The snow all around was churned as if a battle had taken place. The Cubby was rendered into a pile of twisted and broken pieces and several low growing trees were chewed off at their bases, a sign that Carcajou fought viciously with all his might to rid himself of the terrible, painful, demon trap. He located the heavy drag several yards up the trail. This showed the determination and strength the stalwart foe used in its battle against the leg-hold trap. Olaf saw where the chain trailed off from the drag and disappeared under a pile of wind fallen logs from which emanated defiant snarls and hisses.

Realizing that he had the proverbial devil by the tail, Olaf chopped down a sturdy sapling and fashioned it into a killing club. Holding the club at the ready, he gingerly pulled on the chain a little at a time, at the ready for what ever might happen with such an unpredictable and cunning adversary. As he pulled the chain, the animal struggled against being dragged out of his refuge and, all the while, noisily expressed his rage through throaty growls and gnashing of razor sharp teeth. Just as Olaf was feeling confident that he had the enemy conquered, the chain went slack and, like a lightning bolt, the creature catapulted from under the pile, eyes glazed and jaws gaping wide. This tactic took Olaf by surprise and, as he stepped backwards, his heel struck a root, causing him to fall to the ground. In an instant, the wolverine was on top of him, madly thrashing about, trying to get a grip on his throat. Olaf could feel the hot, fetid breath on his cheeks while he desperately used the club to avoid its snapping jaws.

Then, as if from out of thin air, Thor appeared at Olaf's side and heroically fought the crazed animal, giving Olaf the opportunity to roll away from the melee and get to his feet. He saw that the wolverine had a grip on Thor's throat, slowly choking the life from him. In an flash, with all his might, he clubbed the creature between the eyes causing it to release its grip on Thor as it keeled over in the throes of death. A quick examination of the dazed dog showed that there were a few bleeding punctures in the throat area and, other than coughing and gagging, Thor appeared to be out of danger. Olaf figured that the extra thick growth of fur on his ruff and his stocky build had saved him from death. He placed the dog on top of the sled and made it comfortable so that it may settle down. When the realization that Thor had been inches from death's door set in, Olaf broke out in a cold sweat, his body trembled and he began to hyperventilate. He felt that he could never do enough for Thor. Besides being a constant and faithful companion and work partner, the dog now had twice saved his life, this incident and when he and Kyla revived him from a frozen stupor during a storm last winter.

The sun was beginning to set, so Olaf skinned the wolverine before its carcass had a chance to freeze solid. That night at the line camp, Olaf regularly monitored Thor's condition and was relieved when the dog rallied and took some food. They remained an extra day and night at the camp and, during that time, Thor picked up considerably and his energy and interest in things about him were revived. Olaf cleaned the wound marks in the throat area with a saline solution to cut down the chances of infection. On the homeward trip, to preserve Thor's strength, Olaf broke trail with his snowshoes and pulled the loaded sled while the dog followed at its own speed.

Over the course of the next few weeks, Mary's ability to manoeuvre had improved greatly. She made short trips with Olaf and gradually her knee returned to normality. She tended to Thor and kept his wounds clean, thus he came through his ordeal with little mishap. Olaf made several more rounds of the trap line before shutting down for a two week respite, during which they decided to make a visit to their friends at Fox Lake. The March weather was very hospitable and by late afternoon they were descending the trail down to the reserve. As usual, the canine welcoming committee alerted the residents of their arrival and, before they reached Gerald's home, every household doorway was plugged with curious onlookers.

Chief Gerald and Ootah were waiting at the door of their cabin when they pulled abreast of it. Warm and jovial greetings were exchanged between the friends with much hugging and shaking of hands, a trait not usually displayed by many Indians, but the bond of closeness between the couples was strong enough to overcome the native custom of remaining reserved. The Svensons presented their hosts with gifts of tobacco and a small roll of red cotton, a practice that Olaf did not follow before he married but, now, introduced by Mary. The couples stayed up past midnight and talked about many sundry things.

Gerald spoke of Anyiato and how she had failed in her health after Anokee's death. She went into a decline and lost all interest in life and the happenings around her. She and the old Chief had been together constantly for forty five years and were deeply devoted to each other in every respect. This winter her health deteriorated so much that she became extremely frail and seemed to be willing her life away. It is very likely that her spirit will soon leave her body and travel beyond to the happy land to be with Chief Anokee. Olaf and Mary said that they wanted to see her tomorrow if possible and Gerald answered that this would be good.

Kosheena, the ancient care giver and long standing companion to Anyiato, eased her tired body from the rocking chair to respond to the gentle tapping on the door. When she saw who the callers were, her brown, wrinkled face exploded into a wide-mouthed smile and her dark-brown eyes twinkled like stars in the night; surprise and joy overcame her. She firmly grasped the hands of the callers with passionate firmness and, with tearful, happy words bursting forth from her like water over a dam, she beckoned them to enter. The warmth of the dimly lit cabin made it hard to believe the fact that death was imminent. Olaf was taken back to the time over a year ago when he visited old Anokee as he lay on his death bed, exactly where his dying wife now lay.

They stood over her for a few moments observing the serenity of her face as she lay with her eyes closed and lips formed into a hint of a smile. Mary gently held a hand while Olaf stroked her cheeks lightly. Their eyes welled up with grievous tears. Slowly, Anokee's eyes opened, and, with a puzzled expression, peered at the faces of her visitors. At the instant she recognized them, she uttered in the Cree tongue their names, Raven Hair and Gentle

Spirit. Olaf and Mary stayed with her for a while and quietly sat by her side, each cradling a delicate, gnarled hand and smiled at her when ever she forced her eyelids open. Although no words were spoken, Anokee expressed her joy and appreciation by periodically squeezing their hands. They took their leave of her when she drifted off to sleep and conveyed, to Kosheena, that they would return.

During the next two days they visited Anokee twice a day. During their last visit, it was evident, by her shallow breathing, that her time was near. It was that night she passed away peacefully. Kosheena, with the help of Ootah, prepared her body to be stored in the cold shed until the ground thawed in the spring. After the preparation, the body, in its crude wooden casket, was on display for the village people to view followed by a ceremony conducted by Totono. Gerald gave the eulogy. There was much wailing and weeping as Anyiato's body was carried to the storage shed. That evening, a gathering was held in honour of the deceased. Friends, relatives and dignitaries spoke in respect of her person and contributions to the community. Olaf and Mary, as honoured guests, were asked to speak their thoughts and feelings.

Slate coloured clouds scudded across the sky like sailing ships in a race and gradually billowed into black, cumulus masses filled with snow. Olaf had been keeping a wary eye on the changing conditions since they left

Fox Lake. The dogs kept a steady pace over the wind swept lake as they pulled the sled. Mary was comfortably cocooned on the sled and Olaf ran behind, pushing to get through drifts that cropped up. It was not long before the snow started to fall accompanied by a strong, gusty breeze. Fat, wet flakes flung themselves at the travellers and clung to everything, forcing periodic stops to scrape it off. Rather than attempt to make it home under such adverse conditions, Olaf hollered that they will turn up Watson's bay and stop over until the storm passed. Travel was more pleasant with the snow at their backs. Within the hour, they arrived on the doorstep of their friends who were greatly surprised and pleased.

The next day, they left early under a light sky, no wind and more conducive temperatures. The tree branches were heavily loaded with great dollops of snow like icing on a cake. Olaf ran ahead on snow shoes and pounded out a trail over the new fallen snow. They made a stop at noon to brew up a pail of tea to have with the cold bannock and moose jerky. The canines partook in a meal of frozen fish and titbits of bannock. Dusk had stealthily overcome the brightness of the daylight by the time they arrived at the home camp. Within the hour, they had the sled contents unloaded and packed away, the stove lit and the dogs fed. As always, when they have been away on the trap lines, Mary prepared a sumptuous meal to make up for the scant meals they had endured. The rest of the evening was spent in planning their next trip to the trap lines, doing menial tasks, reading and listening to the battery radio. At ten o'clock they prepared for bed. Olaf banked the stove, Mary placed the pot of water on the stove and then they escorted the dogs out for their nightly toilet.

The full moon hovered low in the sky against a backdrop of twinkling stars and was encircled by a multicoloured halo which indicated a change in the weather. They stood arm in arm and marvelled at the beauty before them. The eerie silence of the night was quietly disturbed by the low, melodious hooting of an owl, the far away cry of a lone wolf baying at the moon, the crackling of the fire from within the cabin and the constant snuffle of the dogs searching out the scents of the various animal tracks around the cabin. Intoxicated from nature's elixir, the couple retired to bed and soon succumbed to the demands of their tired bodies and drifted off to sleep amidst the spitting of sparks in the stove and the muffled whimpering of Thor and Kyla in full chase of some animal in their dreams.

CHAPTER TWENTY TWO
NEW FAMILY MEMBERS

The rest of the trapping season went without mishaps. The only thing different was the construction, at Camp One, of a sturdy three walled lean-to topped by a roof of thick willows covered over with overlapping layers of pine boughs, after the fashion of shingles on a house, to prevent snow and rain from filtering through. A sizeable fire pit was built between the lean-to and the heat reflecting wall. Although it was not as complete as the line shack that Carcajou destroyed, it was roomy and comfortable. The shelter had been used on several occasions and on one of those it proved to be a real God-send. Olaf and Mary, on their way home from Camp Number Two with a goodly number of pelts, the last for the season, forged ahead to arrive at the cabin by late afternoon.

The trail was firm and the dogs had no difficulty in sustaining a reasonable speed. They were well beyond Camp Two when a blustery wind suddenly emanated from the north. Tree tops whipped back and forth in a frenzy and old root-weakened trees toppled to the ground. Within minutes the sky was filled with slate-grey clouds which hung low over the trees. A heavy fall of snow erupted from the clouds and enveloped the travellers in a white-out. The visibility was zero and the wet snow was smothering. Olaf was fearful that they would have to stop and shelter on the trail but it was difficult to know where as trees were crashing all around. Thor, in the lead, determinedly forged onward, undaunted by what was happening. Olaf placed Mary in front of him so she could cling to the sled handles and he followed, holding on to the belt of her parka. They doggedly trudged behind the sled like robots.

After what had seemed an eternity, the sled ploughed to an abrupt stop. Thor and Kyla stopped pulling and sat on their haunches, refusing to go any further. Olaf and Mary, panting and gasping, fell to their knees. It was apparent that it would be foolhardy to continue; to fight against such odds would exhaust them to a point of peril. Olaf felt his way forward and freed the dogs from their harness. Thor immediately bolted off the trail and began an incessant chorus of muffled barking. This aroused Olaf's curiosity so he stumbled to where Thor was and, next, Mary heard him whoop and holler. She ploughed her way through the drifts towards the yelling and, to her happy dismay, she saw the hazy outline of the lean-to. Thor's instinctive, canine powers came to the fore once again. The shelter, fortunately, had its back facing the direction from which the storm came, thus the interior was relatively free of snow. Using a snow shoe, Olaf cleared an area for a fire directly in front of the shelter. He got the fuel from the stash of dry kindling and wood stacked in the corner. With frozen and stiff, trembling fingers, he made three clumsy, unsuccessful attempts to light the feathered kindling but, on the fourth try, the struggling match flame prevailed against the wind drafts. Olaf, with cupped hands, coaxed the fire by blowing gentle puffs of air until it took off on its own. Within the hour, Mary had served up, from the frozen packages, a hearty meal of moose stew supplemented with warmed over bannock and hot tea, followed by handfuls of chewy, sweet raisins. The dogs happily worked away at their supper of frozen fish. During the night, the storm petered out like a deflated balloon.

They awoke early to sub-zero conditions. The landscape looked like a cake covered with thick, white icing and the jack-pines were the candles. The black tapestry-sky was sprinkled with twinkling stars and highlighted by a bright, circular moon. The smouldering logs were quickly revived with bits of kindling and in the comfort of a blazing fire, Mary and Olaf ate a scant breakfast of dry bannock washed down with hot tea.

The journey home was extremely trying and exhausting. The trail was deep in snow and it had to be broken for the dogs. Quite often Olaf had to turn back to right the sled when it sank or capsized in the deep snow. The only signs of animal movement were the long holes poked into the thick snow by the stick-like, moose legs and along side of these was the tell-tale evidence of a wolf pack in hot pursuit. It was certain that invariably some of the year olds or calves will end up being the pack's meal.

They were about six miles from home when they stopped to have a light, dry snack. At this point they left the trail and travelled along the lake shore. In the distance, across the expanse of the frozen lake, Olaf spotted a dog team and two persons approaching in their direction. As they got closer, he knew that they were from the Fox Lake Reserve because of the type of toboggan being pulled. When they came along side, Olaf recognized the men. Tom and Joe greeted them in guttural tones and shook their hands. The Indians said that they were on their way home from the post when the storm struck. At the time, they were within a mile of Mary and Olaf's cabin, so they headed for it. They took advantage of the shelter and spent the night, but ate their own food.

The news from the post was that it has been a bad winter with much illness amongst the populace. Ian, the post manager, had a severe bout of influenza and had just recently returned to work, still somewhat weak. The store was opened for a few hours a day by Emma while Ian was convalescing. Ian and Emma send their regards. Because of the frigid cold, the group did not visit long. Two hours saw the Svensons at the door of their wilderness shelter. After much scurrying to unload the sled, get the fire going and the dogs fed, Mary and Olaf were able to sit down to a home cooked meal with all the trimmings. Mary mentioned how thoughtful it was of their visitors to leave a pound of tea as a token of appreciation for the use of the cabin. Lights-out was early because their bodies called for a good night's rest after the gruelling, physical efforts over the past two days. The last sounds heard by Mary and Olaf, as sleep overcame them, was the rhythmic cadence of the dogs' snoring.

Over the next two weeks a lot of needed chores were seen to. Olaf eventually got all the hides cleaned, stretched, dried and bundled. The wood pile was replenished, fish caught, gaps in the wall-chinking that tiny rodents chewed out were repaired, snow shovelled from the roof, sled and the dog harness checked over and reinforced and last but not least, Olaf hunted down and killed a two year old bull moose. Mary, on the other hand, cleaned the cabin, did laundry, mended clothing, knitted socks, made cranberry jam and cooked the meals. After such busy days, they were happy to sit back in the evening to discuss the past events and enjoy the tranquillity. It was during such an evening that Mary shyly imparted to Olaf that it was certain that she was pregnant. Olaf's jaw dropped onto his chest with a plop like a sack of oats and his eyes looked like miniature saucers; he looked entirely flabbergasted.

When the realization of Mary's statement hit home, his countenance changed into a broad smile and from his mouth bubbled happy bursts of laughter. With excited glee, he burst from his chair and grasped her hands and exclaimed how wonderful he felt. Mary reddened slightly and added her excitement to his. She informed him that the baby will possibly arrive in the latter part of June. Olaf asserted that the timing was great because they will go to the post much before her time and Emma could be the mid-wife. In addition to the news about her, Mary stated that Kyla will deliver a litter in the near future. Olaf could not hide the happiness he felt; beads of tears flowed down his ruddy cheeks like tiny rivulets and fell to his lap.

Olaf was now doing the trap-line rounds with Thor. One afternoon as they skimmed their way home across the frozen lake, Olaf surmised that in eight weeks time the ice will be too soft and slushy for travel. They were crossing the last bay near home when he heard the faint drone of an airplane. Shielding his eyes against the glaring sun, he stared off in the direction of the sound and, as if he willed it, the drone changed into a black speck and gradually swelled in size. The plane descended gracefully and gently rested it's skis on the surface and smoothly eased up to the landing. Olaf speeded up to greet Jim when he stepped down from the plane but, as he approached nearer, he saw that it wasn't Jim nor was it his plane.

The pilot stood as still as a statue, waiting for Olaf to reach him. When he introduced himself, there was a depth of sadness in his eyes. He was John Richards, Jim Barnes replacement. About four weeks ago Jim had gone down in a blizzard some where further north and there have been no sightings so it is presumed that he didn't survive. Olaf stood rock still, pale-faced and feeling clammy; his breathing came in short, deep gasps and his chin trembled slightly. He stood as if in a trance and never noticed Kyla jumping up at him nor his wife standing in the doorway. Several minutes passed before he gained his composure. He shook John's hand, introduced himself and invited him to have some refreshment before he took off. They unloaded the supplies and toted them up to the cabin. Olaf introduced Mary to John and explained why Jim was not present. Her face registered disbelief; she stood with enlarged eyes and gaping mouth; she turned away with tears in her eyes and quietly sobbed.

The atmosphere was considerably subdued while they partook of buttered scones and tea. John related that Jim was on his way back to base after dropping supplies off at a mining camp further north and was bringing two miners out with him. Apparently, the weather was ideal for flying when they left the camp in the afternoon. About four o'clock he radioed that they were caught in a sudden snow storm and were experiencing a white-out. The plane was losing altitude due to the heavy build-up of snow and ice on the wings and fuselage. His last radio message was a may-day which said they were going down rapidly in the vicinity of Twin Lakes about sixty miles south of the mining camp. Several of Jim's pilot buddies searched for a week but to no avail. They will resume the search after the snow has gone. Olaf recalled that time when the storm struck from the north and when he and Mary were beset by the blizzard and had to overnight in the lean-to to which Thor so valiantly led them. Also, he and Mary remembered wondering why there was an increase in air traffic over the area shortly after the storm.

Olaf and John loaded the bundles of fur for shipment to the south while Mary made a list of required goods and supplies to be brought in on John's return after the ice leaves the lakes and rivers. Before taking off, John expressed that Jim was well liked and counted on by the people, such as them selves, in the north and how sorry he was that this had happened. The plane slowly taxied to the far end of the bay for take-off space. John momentarily gunned the motor and within minutes the craft was air borne, silhouetted against the setting sun. Two people, with heavy hearts and quiet thoughts, watched the plane fade away into the distance.

The latter, few weeks of the spring season were spent trapping muskrat and beaver from the ponds north of the cabin. The task was not pleasant; he was continuously setting traps in and retrieving carcasses from frigid water and invariably his clothing got wet, causing him to become chilled to the bone. Olaf skinned the animals on the spot so that the sleigh would not become overly heavy for Thor to pull across the slushy snow. Early morning and evening travel was ideal because the wet snow hardened, allowing the sled to glide easily.

The day before he was to close down his operation for the season, Olaf suffered a near fatal mishap. An adult beaver had succeeded in partially pulling the trap-stake out of the mud into deeper water. Olaf could see the drowned animal lying on the bottom and judged that it could be retrieved by using a hooked branch. Carefully placing his rubber-booted feet, he edged his way into the pond until the water reached the top of his footwear. He then groped with the stick until he snagged the leg-trap by the restraining chain. Feeling pleased about his efforts, he slowly backed his way to the shore, but, suddenly, things went awry. His left heel became wedged in the fork of a submerged tree, causing him to lose his balance. Olaf fell backwards and his entire body was immersed under the icy water. His heavy winter clothing soaked up the water to saturation and, frantically, with flailing arms he tried to reach the surface but was pulled down into the depths of the pond. Olaf's mind flashed back to his past life, as is often the case by drowning persons. At the same time he was back-pedalling, seeking firmer footing and, fortunately, just when it seemed that all was over, he felt his feet come up against a tree stuck fast in the mud, allowing him to stand up and get his head above the water. When he surfaced, he sucked in great gulps of air during fits of gasping and coughing.

Gradually his breathing returned to normal and he was able to assess his predicament. He was standing waist deep in the water and his wet clothing weighed a ton on his shivering body. Just ahead of him, within reach, was an overhanging branch of a sturdy willow tree. Grasping it firmly with both hands, he slowly eased himself from the gripping mud and onto the shore. Thor was nervously hopping about and whining pitifully, helpless to aide his master. How the boots stayed on his feet, Olaf could not begin to wonder. As he struggled to pull them off, copious amounts of water and mud poured out all around him. Quickly he unfastened Thor from the sled, donned his boots and high tailed it through the woods to the lean-to about a half mile away. He arrived at the shelter chilled to the bone and desperately rummaged through his baggage for dry matches and clothing. It seemed an eternity before the fire blazed its way through the pile of kindling and dry wood. His teeth chattered like castanets and his body shivered uncontrollably while he peeled off the wet clothing. He stood hugging the fire in his nudity and kept turning himself as if on a vertical spit. When his body felt comfortably dry and warm, he slipped on the clean, warm, dry clothes that were draped before the fire while his wet ones, hung on branches, steamed before the heat.

He and Thor ate their meal in the light of the camp fire. By bed time, his clothing was reasonably dry, but stiff as cardboard. As he lay in his bedroll, Olaf shuddered at the thought of the outcome had he not survived the ordeal at the pond. He felt sick at the thought of not seeing Mary again and guilty that she could have been left alone with their child because of his stupidity. Once again, he was reminded that he was at the mercy of nature that is ever ready to take his life should he let his guard down. With a troubled mind he eventually dropped off, but not without frightening dreams permeating his mind all night.

The near drowning incident delayed him getting home by two days. He did not let it deter him from completing his task, it was the "get back up on the horse that bucked you" attitude. They were homeward bound by late afternoon and found travelling easier due to the hardening of the slush. A brilliant moon was poised just above the tree-tops as they made their way along the final leg of the trail home. The orange glow of a lamp in the window and chimney smoke wafting into the still air were an oasis of warmth and security. He let out a great whoop to alert that he was approaching. Mary yanked open the door, rushed out and flung her arms around Olaf and tightly hugged him to her and tearfully welcomed him home. Once inside, she bombarded him with questions in rapid succession as to why he was late coming home. Mary listened in frozen awe while he recounted the events of the past few days. When he finished, her body involuntarily trembled and tears welled up into her eyes while her hands gripped his in a vice-like hold. It was well into the evening before her composure returned. At bed-time, Olaf snuggled down under the warm, comfy blankets, huddled up to Mary and thought to himself that there was no better feeling in the world at this moment.

Spring subtly crept in and nudged winter out of the way. Bereft of the suffocating ice, the lake swelled to capacity and the river gushed unfettered through the forest and spilled into the lake depositing great amounts of debris and silt at its mouth. As if on cue, birds that had been absent all winter reappeared to settle on the land and waterways, filling the air with their whistling, tweeting, honking and quacking. Within a few weeks the leaf buds on the deciduous trees burst forth, grasses and flowers returned in their summer splendour and animals moved about unrestricted. Olaf and Mary welcomed the relief from the constrictive clutches of the long winter.

One evening, in April, Kyla was restless and paced about the cabin. Mary, realizing that her time to deliver had come, fixed up a bed under the bunk where the dog secluded herself, panting and licking her lips. During the night Olaf and Mary were awakened by the soft, whimpering tones from under the bunk. Excited, they left their bed and raced to peer under the bunk. In the yellow glow of the lamp they witnessed the arrival of the last two babies. The first one had been cleaned by Kyla and as she tended to the others, it wriggled about seeking the warmth of its mother's body. Soon the three newcomers snuggled up against Kyla's stomach and began to voraciously suckle, making contented mewing sounds. The litter was made up of two males and one female, each bearing the colour from both parents, tan, black and white. Thor crawled under the bunk and lay down beside Kyla, occasionally he would sniff and lick the pups, as if to satisfy himself that all was in order. Mary and Olaf returned to their bed, pleased and thankful that it was an uncomplicated birthing.

In the second week of May the sleek, fat pups were romping about, exploring every thing in sight while the parents calmly watched over them. It was on such a day that the Watsons arrived to visit as planned earlier. Josie was completely overwhelmed by the pups; she played with them constantly during their stay. Betty and William were delighted by the news of Mary's pregnancy. William said that he was going to do some extensive repairs to the cabin and add a bedroom for Josie, and they would like to come and visit sometime in September to see the new family member. It was agreed that Betty and Josie would stay with Mary while the men went to the trading post for supplies.

A week prior to Mary's time they canoed to the post. Olaf made several stops along the way so Mary could walk about and stretch to avoid cramping. They had their mug-up at Pierre Deboise's derelict cabin. In the late afternoon, Olaf gently eased the nose of the canoe onto the sandy beach at the Landing. The dogs had hardly touched the ground when a chorus of yowling and baying broke out from the village dogs and a dozen children suddenly emerged, as if from no-where, and descended as a horde down the grassy slope, squealing and laughing with glee, to greet the visitors. There was no lack of helping hands to handle the gear up to the house.

Ian puffed hard on his pipe and grinned broadly as he stood and awaited the group to reach the post. A most joyful reunion took place with much hugging, kissing, handshaking and the odd tear drop flowing down cheeks. They all proceeded to the main house and were greeted by a happy, teary faced Emma, her arms extended wide enough to encompass the entire group. When Ian and Emma were told about Mary's condition, congratulations erupted from the McPhersons. Emma was overjoyed when asked if she would be the mid-wife.

During the evening of their sixth day, Mary's contractions came with regularity, so Emma hustled her into the maternity room and made preparations for the event. Olaf and Ian anxiously paced about the living room and it seemed an eternity before they heard the squalling of an infant's voice, announcing to the world that it had arrived. Both men grinned widely and patted one another on the back. Olaf was beside himself and could not hold back the tears that flowed from his eyes. Emma soon appeared at the door and beckoned to Olaf. With cautious steps he tiptoed into the room and nervously approached the bed. Mary beamed up at him as she pulled back the cover to reveal a tiny, pink and wrinkled bundle. He bent over and kissed his wife and she told him that they have a healthy baby boy. Emma and Ian quietly entered the room to offer their congratulations. The baby began to fidget and smack his lips. This was the cue for Emma to usher the men out so Mary could feed him.

In the fifth week after the birth, Mary and Olaf had the Catholic Priest baptize the baby and christen him Gustav, Frederick, after Olaf's and Mary's fathers. After the church service, a gathering, open to all in the village, was held at the factor's home. Many gifts were presented to the parents in honour of their baby. When Olaf was completely satisfied that all was well with mother and baby, he planned to return home for a few weeks after which he will come back and fetch his family.

Olaf loaded the canoe with dogs, supplies and some building materials, and set off early under a cloudless sky. The longer hours of daylight allowed him to arrive home several hours before sunset. Olaf worked from dawn to dusk every day. He made a child's crib, built a cold storage shed, replaced the stove pipes, stock piled a large supply of fire-wood, repacked chinks between the logs of the cabin, rebuilt the canoe storage deck, and completed a multiple of small tasks that needed attention before the winter came. He was zealous in his approach to the jobs, like a man with a purpose.

The homeward voyage with Mary and Gustav was very relaxed and pleasant. The weather was most cooperative and the few stops made had the flavour of family picnics. The baby's initiation to canoe travel went well. He seemed to enjoy the sway of the craft as it ploughed its way through the small waves. Mary marvelled at the work that Olaf had done and was thoroughly pleased with the crib. There was an atmosphere of happiness and permanence now that the family were in their own home. Mary bustled about fully satisfied in her new role as a mother.

September and October were resplendent with the brilliant colours of the fall season and the warm, hazy days were in keeping with Indian Summer conditions. William arrived with his family and dogs in mid September. The next day he and Olaf left for the post to buy in winter supplies and pick up William's new sixteen foot canoe. They returned four days later, the canoes loaded to within inches of the gunwales. Emma sent several jars of jam to each of the women and Ian presented the men, each, with a bottle of over-proof, Hudson's Bay Rum, purely for medicinal purposes of course. After a one day interval, the Watsons left for home. The new canoe, forest green in colour, held the Watsons and the dogs and the old canoe, in tow, held the cargo. Their journey was pleasant and uneventful, the weather remained comfortably warm.

CHAPTER TWENTY THREE
THE LAST WINTER

In the latter part of September, Olaf spent two days scouting the area west of the cabin with the intent of opening up a new trap line. He hiked along a trail for several miles through a dense forest and eventually came out onto a wide clearing that overlooked a huge beaver meadow holding three large interconnected ponds. A small creek snaked its way down from the distant hills and flowed into the ponds and spilled out over the large dam at the far end and disappeared as a mere trickle into the forest. The dam had created the deep pools; each contained two large beaver houses. Leading off from the pools and towards the trees, like spokes from a wheel, were many narrow channels dug by the beavers and used as canals to float their birch cuttings down to their domed houses. Tell-tale signs of heavy beaver movement, throughout area, were evident. There were many stumps with pointed heads poking up through the debris of wood chips and felled trees. Several of the inhabitants were busy plying their way back and forth, transporting twigs and short logs to their cache below the water. Olaf added this area to his trapping domain.

Within the week he returned with tools and materials and built a sturdy, snug line shack. A circular, fire pit, that was vented through a trap door in the roof, occupied one corner. A sleeping platform, slightly raised above the earthen floor, ran along the wall opposite the fire-place. Two trimmed logs, large in circumference, were destined to be a table and chair. A small window, filled in with a thin square of tanned moose hide, allowed the entry of some diffused light that penetrated the eerie gloom and gave the interior a ghostly aura. Just outside the door he stacked a winter's supply of fire wood and kindling and, as well, stored several armloads inside the shack.

By mid October he had completed readying the other camps so the rest of the month was casual and relaxed. The Indian Summer climate was excellent except for a few rainy days. On many of the warm, hazy days, the family picnicked on the white sandy beaches. Young Gustav and the puppies were growing rapidly and they enjoyed frolicking about and splashing in the pools trapped by the depressions in the rocks. While Mary minded the baby and the pups, Olaf, with the dogs, trolled the bays for the large lake trout that were abound in the deeper waters. Many suppers of trout, barbecued over hot coals, were enjoyed during the tranquil moments before sun-set. On the homeward trip, Gustav and the pups would usually be asleep so the adults took advantage of the solitude and enjoyed the peaceful setting, each with their private thoughts.

One late afternoon as the orange sun was just beginning to dip from sight, John Richards flew in from the north. By the time the plane was unloaded, darkness had set in. Olaf and Mary insisted that John stop over for the night and start his journey afresh in the morning. While Mary and Gustav visited with John, Olaf took the time to read the two letters from Norway. His brother, Sven, wrote that he and Larsen were working the farm entirely on their own as old Gustav was badly afflicted with rheumatoid arthritis. Their mother was doing reasonably well, but she now depends on the assistance of Olga. Also he wrote that Olaf will become an uncle before next Christmas. A tinge of homesickness gripped at his heart as he read the family news. The other letter was from his friend Stefan who wrote that his mother had passed away last summer due to a heart attack and he was now married and the proud father of a one month old boy. He and Marie were so successful with the home farm that they were able to buy out the neighbour's farm and hire two extra hands. When the rest of the household was asleep, Olaf stayed up and wrote replies to his family and Stefan to go out with John in the morning.

After breakfast, Olaf suggested to Mary that they have John fly them all to the post for a visit and then they could canoe back. Mary jumped at the idea and hurriedly packed some belongings while the men lashed the canoe to the pontoon. The Svenson clan boarded the craft with jovial spirits, as happy as an urban family going on a long overdue holiday.

Emma minded and fussed over Gustav in a grandmotherly way while Mary visited the school to meet the new teacher and see her ex-pupils and Olaf was with Ian at the trading post. Ian talked about retiring soon and mentioned that the company would be looking to find a replacement. He strongly urged Olaf to seriously consider applying and, with his recommendation, he was certain that the posting could be his. The prospect of such a situation had some appeal for Olaf. He replied that he would consider the proposition but would need to discuss it with Mary.

The early, ghostly mist that enveloped the lake had lifted considerably when the Svensons pulled away from the landing. Olaf found it easy to propel the canoe across the still, glassy surface, thus they made good time in reaching the old Duboise cabin where they stopped to enjoy Emma's picnic lunch. While young Gustav napped and the dogs lolled about on the hot sand, Olaf told Mary about Ian's suggestion. She carefully replied that there were some very positive aspects to him being the post manager but he must be completely certain that it is something he would like to do and, never the less, knowing that it would be a year or so down the road before Ian retired, he would have the winter to trap and time think about it. The journey home was pleasant until a strong breeze created large waves and a sudden squall soaked them to their skins except for Gustav and the dogs who were placed under a tarpaulin cover. They were extremely pleased that only getting wet was the most uncomfortable part of the trip. The heat from the stove soon dispelled the chilly dampness from them and they settled down to a feast of fried moose steak smothered in wild, fried onions along side of powdered mashed potatoes and boiled, dried peas and topped off with cranberry cake.

Winter set in early and was recorded as one of the coldest since 1910 when everything virtually came to a standstill. The older generations of Indians and trappers talked about the great number of deaths from influenza and pneumonia and trapping fell to an all time low. Constant winds and falling snow made travel next to impossible. Some trappers who did not get in an ample supply of deer and moose meat and provision from the post had died of starvation or had frozen to death. The Fox Lake Reserve lost over a third of its population, mainly young children and elderly. Fortunately, Olaf, had a plentiful supply of store provisions and the storage shed was well stocked with frozen meat and fish so his family did not suffer due to the restrictions of the deplorable winter conditions.

When he went out on the trap lines, Olaf left the dogs at home because the deep snow hindered their movements. He made better time alone on snowshoes. One afternoon, burdened with a pack of pelts, he was labouring along a trail that led him through a forest of mixed pine and popular when an eerie feeling momentarily seized him. He quickly dismissed it, blaming it on the stillness of the woods, the early dusk and the phantom shadows that created imaginary movements of ghost like creatures. His snowshoes ploughed effortlessly through the deep, soft snow as his strong legs worked steadily like pistons. Ten minutes had passed, since he had the eerie feeling, when he felt the need to rest so he slumped his backside down on to a fallen tree.

Casually looking around, he momentarily caught, from the corner of his right eye, a fleeting glimpse of blurry movements amongst the trees. He trained his eyes in that direction and soon there boldly emerged, from out of the shadows, four, huge timber wolves that stealthily moved towards him, cautiously watching his every move through yellow, slit eyes. As if rehearsed, the group broke away and formed a semi-circle around him and calmly sat on their haunches and leisurely studied him as if they had all the time in the world. Olaf tried to convince himself of the theory that wolves rarely attack humans, but, with the severe winter conditions, this may be an exception if they have not been successful in hunting.

Dusk was quickly turning to darkness and he knew that some decisive and well calculated action on his part needed to be executed immediately. Slowly he slithered has hand towards the rifle and deftly removed it from his shoulder, slid back the bolt and shoved a bullet into the chamber. From the corner of his eyes, he noticed the two wolves flanking him were edging closer and low, throaty growls emanated from within their deep chests while the other two quietly stayed their ground. It was obvious to him that these beasts were serious in making him their much desired meal. Suddenly the side pair rushed in at him as if catapulted like launched missiles. In a flash, Olaf spun towards the closest and fired from the hip, the bullet smashed into its chest and exploded outward, creating a huge hole at the base of its spine. Having no time to breech a second bullet, he quickly shifted the gun and grasped it by the barrel and with all his might, whilst it was airborne, he swung the rifle and knocked the other wolf to the ground. It fell at his feet, gasping and spluttering with a crushed larynx from the heavy throat chop it received from the rifle butt. Immediately the spectator wolves bolted into the semi-darkness and scurried away like two mice being chased by a cat. The bludgeoned wolf lay on the ground gasping for air and its entire body involuntarily twitching. Olaf stepped over to where it lay and hastened its death by shooting it through the heart. Leaving the dead animals where they lay, he trudged homeward through the darkness.

Olaf did not venture out to the trap lines for about three weeks as the big chill lasted well into January making it unbearable for man or beast to get around. It was just as well that he was not away from home because Gustav came down with a fever and a croup which took most of Mary's time and energies to nurse him. Olaf took the strain off Mary by doing the cooking, cleaning, maintaining the fire, hauling water and feeding the dogs. Both parents were anxious over their son and catered to his every need. Eventually, after nearly two weeks, Gustav's condition improved and by the end of the third week he rallied and was himself again. Gradually the thermometer readings began to climb and each succeeding day's temperature climbed closer to the freezing mark where it hovered well into February.

Olaf made a week's journey into his new trapping area west of the cabin and brought home a bundle of ten beaver hides, three being prime and blanket size. One day, about noon, he was sitting as still as a statue over the open water hole, jigging for fish. A white fish and three large trout lay on the frigid snow close by. The sun was high in the sky and the air was comfortably warm. He was deeply engrossed with fishing when the quietness in his head was interrupted by the faint drone of an airplane in the far distance. He stood up and slowly scanned the clear blue sky and soon spotted a dark dot. Intently he gazed at it as it slowly emerged into plain view. When the plane touched down and taxied towards the landing, he recognized it to be John. After the salutations, the supplies and mail were unloaded and toted up to the cabin.

Mary warmly greeted John, Gustav gurgled and smiled at him and a group of excited pups jumped up and down around his legs and almost tripped him. John had time for a quick cup of tea and a sandwich before heading out further north to the miners' camps. He told them that there had been news from the north that a group of Indians on a hunting expedition came across Jim's plane. Apparently, when they went down, the plane smashed into the side of high bluff at the edge of a small lake and tumbled down into a deep depression where the snow had covered it over. It was last week when the remains of the three bodies were brought out. A coroner and a Mounty accompanied the pilot and two helpers to make out the official report on the accident and bring out the remains.

The thick ice on the lake had rotted considerably by the end of May and slush ice hugged the shore line. The Grass River had stayed in full spate for two weeks, spewing water, ice and debris into the lake. Pockets of snow, trapped in depressions and dotted throughout the forest were the only remnants of the harsh winter that had been. Spring had finally arrived. The sharp cries of the saucy magpies and the raucous croaks of the bold ravens, that stayed all winter, were now in competition with the choruses from sparrows, finches, whip-poor-wills, red breasted black birds, ducks, geese, loons and many other species of birds. Pesky hordes of mosquitoes and black flies soon made their appearance to bedevil man and beast. In the late afternoon and evening, smudge pots were so arranged that a pall of smoke hovered over the cabin area like a fog which discouraged the biting pests from lingering and allowed the family to sit out and enjoy the serenity of the late afternoon and early evening.

One warm evening, while sitting on the porch, Mary expressed her fears and concerns to Olaf about him continuing as a trapper now that he has a family to consider. She confessed that she dreads when he is away from home, ever thinking that he may not come back due to an accident that could take his life. When she accompanied him before Gustav came, it did not bother her as she was there to help and look after him. She would feel more secure and relaxed if he would possibly consider giving up trapping and apply for Ian's job. Olaf sat quietly and gazed over the mirror-like surface of the lake and blew clouds of blue smoke into the evening air.

Several minutes passed before he turned to her, looked into her large, hazel eyes and spoke. Since they had married, he related, he had often thought to himself about the situation into which he had brought her and wondered if it was fair to expect that she would be happy and content. Gustav's coming on the scene put things into a different perspective. Living at the post, where there would be the security of a steady income, a nice comfortable house, company for Mary and eventually schooling for the boy, is what he would like very much. In fact, he said, even though he hadn‘t discussed it with her, Angus was told to go ahead and submit his name as a candidate for the job. He didn't want tell her until he knew if the job was his but the way Angus spoke, it was a certainty that it would be. Mary leaned over and hugged him closely and, when she looked at him, her beaming smile presented a picture of utmost happiness.

As pre-planned on the last visit, the Watsons appeared early in June. William and John would go to the post to buy supplies and the women would stay behind with the dogs. That evening Olaf told the Watsons that if he got the position as factor of the post, they would be giving up the trap line and cabin and move to Hall's Landing. Ian, he said, should have an answer for him when they go there tomorrow. William and Betty expressed their happiness for them and wished them luck and hoped that he would get the job. They all agreed that they wouldn't be so far apart and they would still be able to visit back and forth. The two men left at the break of day. The weather conditions were excellent and when they arrived at the landing, late that afternoon, they both agreed that the travel time seemed quite short.

They spent two days at the post and left in the morning

of the fourth day. They arrived at the cabin at dusk. Had it not been for the stiff breeze and foot high waves they had to paddle against, they could have been home by mid-afternoon. Within the hour the supplies were stowed safely within the cabin and the canoes, placed upside down, were securely moored in case the weather turned for the worse.

During the evening meal, a great deal of excited dialogue went on among the adults about the future of the Svensons. Olaf had announced earlier that Angus confirmed that his appointment as the Post Factor had been sanctioned by the Hudson's Bay Office in Winnipeg. The company wants him to spend six months working with Angus before he retired. Also, Olaf stated that this summer they were going to go outside and visit Mary's parents and then travel to Norway to see his family. His statement created an excited flutter within the group. Mary was beside herself with happiness. She jumped from her chair and threw her arms around Olaf and hugged him tightly while rivulets of tears drained down her cheeks. Betty and William quietly chortled at Mary's display of happiness while brushing away tears from the corners of their eyes. When Mary regained her composure, Olaf declared, in a somewhat authoritative voice, that there was a lot to be discussed. He announced that he had a proposal to put before the Watsons. Without hesitation, he suggested that they move in to this cabin and take over the trap lines as established, seeing that their place is smaller and William's area is slow in recovering after the devastating fire. Besides, this place would go to ruin in no time without a tenant and they would only be less than a day's journey from the post. It would please him and Mary to no end if they would accept. Taken by surprise, Betty and William looked at one another, speechless and, seeming at first, not believing what they heard. After what seemed an eternity, William spoke. He cleared his throat and said that he and Betty would be very happy to accept. Olaf sprung from his seat and grasped William's hand and shook it vigorously, finalizing the arrangement.

CHAPTER TWENTY FOUR

NEW BEGINNINGS

Olaf and his family were away for three months and during that time the Watsons had moved into the cabin on Wekusko Lake and Ian had built a cosy log cabin on the lake shore close to the post. When the Svensons returned, they were able to take up residence in the factor's house immediately. Thor, Kyla and the pups, who were under Ian's care, greeted them in their excitable and happy canine way, leaping up at them whilst yipping and whining. While Olaf was learning the ropes of running the trading post, Mary was busy setting up their home with the furnishings purchased in Winnipeg. By the end of March, Angus gracefully stepped down and handed the reigns over to Olaf, conferring upon him the official title as Factor of the Hall's Landing Trading Post.

Olaf enjoyed being a post manager but there were times when he longed to be out trapping. He missed the solitude of the forests and pitting his wits against the vagaries of nature. When these thoughts surfaced he told himself that the life he knew then was not practical as they were expecting their second child and he had to create a safe and stable environment for the family.

He was kept abreast about the happenings in his old area through the moccasin telegraph and from talking with his friends who came from Fox Lake to trade. One piece of news that made Mary and Olaf extremely sad was that Gerald and Ootah lost their only son of ten months to a severe bout of influenza. The sickness was fatal to several other children as well as three of the eldest members of the tribe. The sadness was made more profound by their own parental concerns and fears of losing a child. They knew that Gustav and their expectant child were as susceptible to sickness as any other child.

The Svensons made a visit to the Watsons while Angus looked after the post. The balmy, hazy Indian Summer climate made their journey pleasant in every way. Gustav's childish curiosity about everything he saw amused his parents to no end. One instance was when Olaf was steering towards a spit of land, where they planned to stop for a mug-up, they saw a pack of four wolves tearing at and devouring great chunks of flesh from a young deer. Gustav was fascinated at the sight and stared with eyes nearly as big as saucers. He pointed at the wolves and uttered that the doggies were bad. The family beached the canoe further down the lake and enjoyed a quiet noon-time lunch.

They stayed with the Watsons for three days and,

on one of these days, Olaf went with William for a hike around the line to Camp Number One. Olaf showed him around and explained where the best places were to set traps. To further assist him, he drew a map of the other areas. The line camps were in good repair and all the equipment had been left in the huts. Upon parting, it was agreed that the Watsons will come and spend the Christmas and New Years festivities at the post.

Winter arrived at the end of November with temperatures plummeting and heavy snowfalls. Olaf had been very busy seeing to outfitting the trappers and Indians as well as providing groceries to the community families. It was a busy but happy way of life for Olaf and his family. Gradually, the yearning to be out on the trap lines left him and he dedicated himself to the task of factor. He made a flying trip out to Winnipeg to meet the company officials. He was busy with meetings and visitations to the suppliers' warehouses in order to familiarize himself with what they carried and to purchase goods for the store. Being in the city was not Olaf's greatest joy. He missed the vastness and quietness of the northland's green forests, pristine lakes, flowing streams and rivers and the animal life. Thus, it was with great happiness that he boarded the plane for the trip home. It was reminiscent of the first time he flew over the landscape, except, this time, it was blanketed under great depths of snow. He felt a great sense of belonging in the wilderness and, though he missed

Norway, he knew that he would never willingly trade this way of life. Everything has now been fulfilled for him in his life, his family, his job, his close friends and having had the experience of being a trapper. He was jolted from his thoughts by the sudden step-down and sharp banking of the plane as it came in to land. He looked down upon the cluster of tiny cabins and saw white plumes of smoke belching forth and patches of orange light from the coal oil lamps piercing the dusk through small windows. His home coming was a joyous occasion. There was so much to tell as well as presenting gifts to Mary and Gustav.

Within several months of settling in, the Svensons were blessed with a healthy girl; old Emma taking on the role as mid-wife again. The babe was the spitting image of her mother. She had beautiful hazel eyes, raven hair and very fair skin. Helga Louise, named after the grandmothers, was an adorable, cuddly baby. Gustav took a delighted interest in his sister and spent many hours amusing her.

In the fiftees the demand for fur began to wane as there was not the demand for pelts, only the rich could afford the luxury of fur garments, thus fur trading became less lucrative and many trappers left the trap lines to earn a living down south. The Hudson's Bay Company closed down most of their smaller posts, Hall's Landing being one of those. Olaf faced this reality with a practical alternative to giving up and leaving. The community of several hundred people, he reasoned, will still need food and supplies and the government still maintained a police force and provided schooling, medical care and welfare subsidy to the native people. Thus, he obtained the post store and company house for next to nothing from the Company and entered into the realms of a free trader and merchant. Over the years, his store, Svensons' Merchandising, became reasonably successful and provided a good living and the satisfaction of being his own boss again.

Olaf, being of a restless nature, wanted to direct his energies into a new venture. It was the era of the well-to-do business men wanting a get-away adventure from the humdrum of city work and life. So, he associated himself with John Richards, now pilot-owner of Northern Airways, in a business adventure that catered to hunters and fisherman by offering holiday adventure deals for fishing and hunting. The overall cost to the clients included air flight, full accommodation with meals and guides. Olaf built a huge pine-log lodge to house and feed the sportsmen. The operation was a much needed boost to the local economy in that resident Indians were hired to construct the lodge and landing wharf, to hunt and fish for the menu and be guides. The fly-in fishing and hunting camp was a huge success, thus making Olaf a man of more than modest means.

It was at this time that William Watson made the

decision to give up trapping and planned to move his family back to the United States. Olaf offered him the position as manager of the holiday camp operations because he needed a reliable person to run it while he ran the post store. William accepted and he moved his family to the Landing and took up residence in the priest's, old house. Now, Betty and Josie had a more defined way of life in that they had the companionship of Olaf's family and the people of the community rather than the loneliness of isolation.

Over the years the holiday-camp part of the business was expanded to include six cabins for families seeking a wilderness holiday and the store was expanded to handle the needs of the summer tourists. Mary and Betty were in charge of the lodge. They hired local Indian ladies for cleaning, laundry, cabin maids, kitchen help and cooks.

The years plodded on one by one and many changes occurred. Old Angus and Emma had passed on, Josie and Gustav attended school in the south, an Anglican Church was built, Olaf's old cabin was refurbished and used as an outer camp for moose hunters, there were three planes a week, regular mail service and bi-monthly doctor and Public Health nurse visits. Under a Federal Government relocation program, the Fox Lake Band was moved to and housed at Hall's Landing in newly built, two bed-room dwellings, thus swelling the population considerably.

Except for the odd trip out for a holiday or a visit to the

family in Norway and Idaho, the Svensons and Watsons spent most of the next thirty years at Hall's Landing. On the other hand, their children, in their early adult years, moved to Winnipeg where they pursued their careers and settled down with their own families.

As sorry as they were to leave Hall's Landing, William and Betty eventually moved back to Idaho to farm the land that his father had bequeathed to him, leaving Olaf to carry on by himself. The time for Olaf to bow out of the Mercantile and Tourist Trade arrived when the crippling disease of rheumatoid arthritis, which had worsened over the years, took hold to the point that he could not function physically well enough to run the business properly. Thus, Olaf had no option but to quit working so he sold the business to two young enterprising Indians who worked for him during their summer vacations from college in Winnipeg, consequently having a lot of knowledge and understanding which enabled them to take over the reins without any serious interruption to the services provided under Olaf's administration.

Two years later, Olaf, at the age of eighty three, passed away quietly in his sleep, thus ending the era of a courageous, stalwart and gentle man. The Fox Lake Band honoured "Gentle Spirit" with a special Indian ceremony and memorial gathering reserved only for Chiefs and highly respected tribal members. The Chief of the Band, Gerald's nephew, echoed the condolences of all the Indian people and stated that "Princess Raven Hair" will always have a special place in their hearts and the memory of their brave brother will live on forever amongst them. He was buried under a towering maple tree in the white, picket-fenced cemetery on the hill overlooking the lake and forests beyond. The inscription, "Olaf Svenson, Gone But Not Forgotten", was deeply carved into the wooden head piece and adorned with a wrought iron cross.

Mary moved to Winnipeg to be near her children and grandchildren and when she died at the age of seventy five years she was buried next to Olaf.

ABOUT THE AUTHOR

Arthur Joseph Fry was born in Windsor, Ontario, Canada. He graduated from the University of Calgary with a Teaching Degree and a Master's Diploma in Educational Administration. His first teaching assignment was in an isolated community called Moose River located in Northern Ontario. The only access was by rail once a week or chartered aircraft. He was in charge of a one-room school and taught Cree Native and several Non-Indian status children from Grades One to Nine. As well as being the Principal Teacher his duties encompassed that of being the School Nurse, Student Advisor and janitor. Moose River was a small native settlement that boasted a saw mill, a Free Trader's Post managed by a Norwegian and his Cree wife, a school and a railway track maintenance centre. The main outlets for employment were the saw mill, railway gang and fur trapping His interactions with the local population allowed him insight into the methods of fur trapping and trading, activities in which he took an interest.

"Traps and Pelts" is his first fictional novel based on the information gleaned through discussions with Cree trappers, seeing a few of their line camps and social visits to the settlement.

Printed in the United Kingdom
by Lightning Source UK Ltd.
PP531100001B/1